Picturing Christmas

Picturing Christmas

Jason F. Wright

and Sterling Wright

SWEETWATER
BOOKS

An Imprint of Cedar Fort, Inc.
Springville, Utah

This is a work of fiction. The characters, names, incidents, places, and dialogue are products of the author's imagination and are not to be construed as real. The opinions and views expressed herein belong solely to the author and do not necessarily represent the opinions or views of Cedar Fort, Inc. Permission for the use of sources, graphics, and photos is also solely the responsibility of the author.

ISBN 13: 978-1-4621-2152-6

Published by Sweetwater Books, an imprint of Cedar Fort, Inc.,
2373 W. 700 S., Springville, UT 84663
Distributed by Cedar Fort, Inc., www.cedarfort.com

Names: Wright, Jason F., author. | Wright, Sterling, 1962- author.
Title: Picturing Christmas : a novella / Jason F. Wright, with Sterling
   Wright.
Description: Springville, UT : Sweetwater Books, an imprint of Cedar Fort,
   Inc., [2017]
Identifiers: LCCN 2017033162 (print) | LCCN 2017034452 (ebook) | ISBN
   9781462128617 (ebook) | ISBN 9781462121526 (hardcover : alk. paper)
Subjects: LCSH: Women photographers--Fiction. | New York (N.Y.), Setting. |
   LCGFT: Christmas fiction. | Novellas.
Classification: LCC PS3623.R539 (ebook) | LCC PS3623.R539 P53 2017 (print) |
   DDC 813/.6--dc23
LC record available at https://lccn.loc.gov/2017033162

Cover design by Jeff Harvey
Cover design © 2017 by Cedar Fort, Inc.
Edited and typeset by Erica Myers

Printed in the United States of America

10 9 8 7 6 5 4 3 2 1

Printed on acid-free paper

To Kodi, who has Christmas dancing in her eyes all year long.   —Jason

To Ann, who took me to Manhattan on our first real date many years ago. That's where I fell in love with her and the city. —Sterling

Other books by Jason F. Wright

The James Miracle
Christmas Jars
The Wednesday Letters
Recovering Charles
Christmas Jars Reunion
Penny's Christmas Jar Miracle
The Seventeen Second Miracle
The Cross Gardener
The Wedding Letters
The 13th Day of Christmas
The James Miracle: 10th Anniversary Edition
Christmas Jars Journey
A Letter to Mary

Prologue

Aubrey stood next to the Christmas tree, both hands on her stomach. She closed her eyes and breathed in the scents of the first real tree she remembered having in years. The massive Frazier fir was decorated from the velvet skirt around its trunk up to a red glass ball about two feet from the top. The rest would have to wait until her taller helper arrived.

She stepped back and admired the cozy Christmas corner she'd created. The tree was flanked on either side by some of her favorite Christmas photographs. Most of them brought back very fond memories. A couple could make her cry, if she let them.

One photo stood out among them all. It was a picture so familiar, she could close her eyes and see every color and dot. She could smell the sweetness of the time and place it was shot. She could feel the camera in her hand. Unlike many of her other photos, this one had never been published or won any awards. Still, it was perhaps her favorite photo of the countless she'd snapped through the years.

The simple shot reminded her that a little girl's face can light the world.

She rubbed her stomach again and wondered how her child would experience Christmas. Would Aubrey be able to maintain the magic? What would the family pictures look like?

Her belly let out a rumble to remind her that she was constantly hungry these days. Aubrey straightened one of her pictures, then straightened it again, and finally stepped back and decided it was perfect just a little bit sideways.

As she admired her work, her stomach spoke up once again. "I know, I know. So, what sounds good? Cold pizza?" She smiled and pretended to listen. "Me too."

228 Days to Christmas

She looked across the audience, her dark brown eyes the lens of a mental camera. She'd become so immersed in her final project that life appeared before her as a series of still images. Each shot was composed and balanced, the scene divided into nine squares. Her head turned and tilted subconsciously to make interesting objects line up at imaginary intersections. The tassel of her cap drifted in and out of her view like a camera strap slipping in front of a lens.

She looked at her parents.

"Aubrey Porter," the dean droned.

Before turning to accept her diploma, she blinked and stored a picture in the part of her brain that held memories that never faded. She processed the image while continuing across the stage and back to her seat.

It was a good picture of a sad couple. They sat in folding chairs attached to one another. But Claire and Randall were separately outlined by the brilliant mid-morning sun as it rose behind them. Somehow, they managed not to touch each other at all. Even the sharp shoulder of his jacket and her designer scarf seemed to repel one another.

His knees pointed slightly right.

Hers slightly left.

A light pole stood at the edge of the parking lot thirty feet behind them. In Aubrey's mental picture, it would divide the space between their tilted heads. The picture told a long story.

She watched the rest of her class march up to collect their diplomas and shake the dean's hand while turning toward a hundred cameras. Every picture would be the same, except for the face framed between the cap and the collar of the gown. Each face would have two eyes, a nose, and a mouth. Each mouth would be turned up in a smile. Yet, Aubrey knew that a good photographer could capture something unique about each person. She wondered what an honest picture of her face would say right now.

In just a few minutes—the dean was in the Ws—Aubrey would leave the safe sea of black gowns to navigate the choppy waters surrounding her parents. She'd been caught completely by surprise when her mother called her at the beginning of the semester to tell her about the divorce. "Your father and I can't be together anymore, dear. It's been a long time coming. We'll talk when you come home at break."

As she steeled herself for what she was sure was going to be an awkward graduation dinner, she cursed herself for not recognizing the signs. Her father had always spent more time at work than most dads. Still, when Aubrey was little, he seemed happy when he was home or out with his family. Her mother was happy too, and didn't seem to mind the role of Super Mom. As the family aged, Dad's smiles became less frequent and his curt manner more pronounced. Mom's smiles grew more forced and her eyes began to look old and tired.

Twenty-two-year-old Aubrey recognized now what her younger, self-centered version could not see. Claire and Randall Porter had drifted apart over the years, only loosely lashed together by their daughter. Four years ago, their final reason to stay married got in the new Honda her father bought her and drove away to college.

The dean's final "Good luck, graduates" pulled her back to the ceremony. She put on her "thanks for everything" face, tossed her cap into the air, and rushed to greet her parents.

❧

The only way Randall Porter would ever eat at McDonald's was if they started offering valet parking. As far back as Aubrey could remember, the Porters used the service as the minimal requirement for a good restaurant. They would eat elsewhere in a pinch, but Randall always found something to criticize. The place they pulled up to for graduation dinner had to be the only restaurant in Albuquerque with an honest-to-goodness valet. Aubrey unsuccessfully tried to steer her parents to one of the great restaurants she'd discovered while at school. "This is a special night," her father had said. "We're going to a special restaurant."

Claire didn't say a word. Instead, she sent Aubrey a familiar glance of exasperation.

"I'm really not dressed for a fancy place," Aubrey said as she looked down at her shorts and sandals. The casual, cool attire was perfectly acceptable under a graduation gown on a ninety-degree day, but not for a five-star Italian restaurant.

"Nonsense. Just act like you belong and you'll belong." He pressed a ten into the hand of a teenager with a flat top and a shirt one size too big. Aubrey noticed that Randall didn't even look back at the car. He would normally ensure the valet treated the vehicle with care and respect.

Ah, rental, she thought.

Claire and Randall had flown up—separately— from Dallas for graduation. When Aubrey picked her college, The University of New Mexico seemed like a perfect choice. It had excellent art and photography programs and sat in the college kid sweet spot: close enough to home for the occasional visit, but far enough away to avoid drop-ins by the parents. Right after the divorce, she wondered if she'd have been better off going to Yale or one of the prestigious New York schools. It didn't matter in the end. The only difference the split made was that her few trips back "home" included two stops instead of one. Claire came out to New Mexico once each semester and Randall visited one time during sophomore year to inspect the off-campus apartment he helped Aubrey rent.

The hostess took them back to their table. Randall sat and picked up the menu. Aubrey was about to sit when Claire chirped, "Just get us some water. We need to go to the ladies' room."

Randall nodded without looking up.

"I'm so proud of you, sweetheart." Claire put one arm around Aubrey as they walked through the restaurant together.

"Thanks, Mom."

"It's been hard."

Aubrey couldn't tell if her mother was talking about school, Aubrey being away at school, life after the divorce, or life in general. "For all of us," she answered.

That covers everything.

Claire touched her daughter's cheek gently with the back of her hand before reaching for the door handle.

When they got back to the booth, Randall was sipping a glass of wine with his eyes closed. "Salad's on the way. I ordered a little of everything so everyone will be happy." He put down his glass and looked at Aubrey. She'd sat directly across the table from him. "I loved your project, by the way."

"Thanks," she answered, wondering if he'd ever even looked at it.

"Who would have thought such simple, everyday objects could be so beautiful."

Wow. He did *look at it.* "Thanks," she said, this time with more enthusiasm.

"So, now what? Tell us about that great job you just landed."

Aubrey was a terrible liar, but she'd mastered the art of the half-truth. "It's a great opportunity in New York City. A sorority sister knows someone who writes for an online fashion magazine. She hooked me up with the staff photographer and he liked my work."

"New York, huh? I'm not a big fan of the Big Apple."

"I know, Daddy." She hated it when the word *Daddy* slipped out. She also hated it when he pretended to hear something for the first time when it was more like the fifth or sixth.

"Expensive too. Is this job going to cover your costs?"

"It should."

"Mmm-hmm." He tilted his head down and examined her as if looking over a pair of reading glasses. He was about to continue as the first course arrived. The smell of fresh bread, vinegar, and garlic made Aubrey's stomach growl and reminded her how long it had been since breakfast.

"Wait!" she said as Randall reached for a piece of bread. She took out her phone and commanded her mother, "Hop out and skoosh in with Dad." Aubrey slid out after her and knelt on the seat of the next booth, resting her phone on top of the divider. The wine must have started working because Randall let Claire sit right next to him. "Now, take a really deep breath," Aubrey said. "Smell all that Italian awesomeness." Warm, natural smiles appeared on both faces as their brains processed the scents. "One more. Just keep looking forward." She stepped into the aisle and took another picture. Half the restaurant was now staring at them, but Aubrey was used to it.

"Always a shutter bug." Randall looked around and flushed a bit. "Sit down and eat." He broke off a piece of bread and dipped it in olive oil. "And no more pictures for a while."

While they ate, the trio enjoyed talking about nothing in particular, and Aubrey was pleased that her parents had put away the knives long enough to enjoy the occasion. Later, while they were waiting for the car, Randall put his arm around Aubrey and said, "Come take a little walk with me."

They strolled along the sidewalk in front of the restaurant and enjoyed the cool evening breeze. "I have a present for you."

"Okay," Aubrey said, her default response when nothing else came to mind.

Randall pulled a plastic card from his shirt pocket. "It's an ATM card attached to a Wells Fargo account."

"Okay."

"Don't go crazy, but don't worry about overdrafts, either, if you know what I mean."

"Thanks, Daddy, but I don't know what you mean."

"Your mother could have taken me to the cleaners in the divorce, but she didn't. I don't know why, but she didn't. So this is my way of paying some penance, I guess, and saying congratulations and I'm proud of you." He furrowed his brow, the streetlight casting black shadow stripes across his forehead. "Dang it, that came out wrong."

"I don't need your money, Dad."

"I know, sweetie, just consider it a safety net. A graduation present safety net."

"I don't know . . ."

He turned back toward the restaurant. "Either you take it or the valet is going to get the best tip of his life."

220 Days to Christmas

Aubrey stood in the bedroom doorway and looked at her childhood. Directly across from her hung a huge framed Ansel Adams print, not of a majestic mountain range or wind-swept dune, but of the Los Angeles freeways. She got it when she was a high school junior and had begun to look forward to going out into the world. It hung where it did because she needed to cover what was left of a Cold Play poster she'd glued to the wall during middle school. She'd been terrified when the temporary adhesive turned out to be not-so-temporary. The larger Adams photo helped avoid a cold scolding from her father.

She scanned the room and realized that her mother had cleaned and straightened it without really changing a thing. The bed was crisply made—which was rare when Aubrey was growing up—but it still had the same comforter she'd slept under throughout her high school years. The books that had been precariously stacked on the ends and edges of her shelf were now dusted and lined up neatly, and, Aubrey guessed, in alphabetical order. It was her room, but not quite. It looked as if archeologists had uncovered an ancient teenager dwelling and tried their best to reconstruct it.

Aubrey felt Claire walk up close behind her as she put her hand on her shoulder. "I know you got this ready for me, Mom, and I appreciate your letting me not stay here."

"I think I understand, sugar. This is a kid's room. You're all grown up."

"I don't know about that." She paused. "But thanks for letting me use the guest room."

"It's just great to have you here. Randall didn't think you'd want to stay with him, and I wondered if you wanted to be with me after . . ."

"You can say 'divorce,' Mom. It happens to lots of people."

"It wasn't supposed to happen to us, Aubrey. I tried so hard for it not to happen to us."

Aubrey wanted to hug her mother and tell her it was okay. That life would go on. That it wasn't Claire's fault. She wasn't sure yet whose fault it was, if any-one's. But, she wasn't convinced that everything was going to be okay. She did know that life would go on, but didn't know what that life was going to look like.

"You know, I think I'll unpack and take a little nap." She forced a tiny smile and wheeled her suitcase along the shiny oak floor of the hallway. She probably wouldn't sleep, but she needed some time to dry the tears she knew were on the way.

175 Days to Christmas

Living in the guest room instead of her old bedroom was the right call, Aubrey decided. After just a couple weeks at home, she felt inertia pull her to toward old habits and old acquaintances. But, between Claire's overzealous efforts to keep Aubrey occupied, Randall's complete absence, and a different set of walls to look at, she was able to navigate the summer as an aspiring young professional rather than a kid back from college.

She did spend time with a few high school friends, but her two closest friends had moved from Texas while Aubrey was in New Mexico. They stayed in touch over the internet, but posting an update wasn't the same as sharing a look or a giggle across the room.

She had 610 Facebook friends, and nobody to talk to. Aubrey felt more alone than at any time since her first semester at college.

Claire seemed to sense her daughter's loneliness. She tried to be both friend and mother, often cleverly arranging together time. There were lots of shopping trips and dinners out. They played the occasional game of scrabble or rummy. Claire even let Aubrey teach her how to play Angry Birds on her iPad.

On a cooler-than-normal evening—it was under ninety degrees outside—Claire asked Aubrey for help going through the garage. "Your father says he took everything he wanted, but there is still a lot of man stuff out there. Let's see what we can give away, burn, or just pitch."

The "man stuff" turned out to be a red metal box full of hardly used household tools, an old golf club that Randall used to hit Whiffle balls with in the backyard, and the lawn mower the neighbor kid used to mow the grass with. The neighbor kid had to be over twenty years old now, and a professional lawn service had been taking care of the property for a long time. "I wonder why Dad never got rid of this mower. Did you ever see him use it?"

"Once or twice just after he bought it. He probably left it just so I'd have to figure out what to do with it."

"Maybe you should hold on to it in case you have to have someone come and mow. Keep the tools too. You never know when you might need to tighten something. Or bang on something. Or something on something." She looked at the toolbox and thought she was being funny. But then she looked over at Claire. "Oh, Mom, what's wrong?"

"I'm sorry." She pressed the heel of her hand against the corner of her eye. "It's just the lawn and the house and the million other things I never had to worry about before."

"Come on, Mom, you can take care of yourself."

"Of course I can, dear. Randall never did any of that stuff himself, anyway. I would tell him what was broken and he would call the person who fixed it. But now I don't have the middle man."

"I see." Aubrey didn't.

"Sometimes, I miss the middle man."

"Mom, you don't need him. We don't need him. Do you think he is at his place looking at your picture wishing you would call and tell him the sink is stopped up?"

"Probably not."

"No. Now come on, let's see if we can find anything of his to break. Or burn." She looked at the labels on the bins and boxes that lined the shelves along one wall. "Dishes, cleaning supplies, gardening stuff, touch-up paint . . . what's this one?" She slid a big, green plastic bin to the edge of its shelf and eased it to the floor.

Claire lit up. "That must be the missing Christmas bin! I moved all the decorations to the attic a few years ago, but I knew some things weren't there." She rushed over and knelt on the floor, ignoring the fact that her bare knees were resting on concrete.

Aubrey sat cross-legged across from her, the bin dividing the space between them. This close to the floor, the garage smelled more mechanical and oily. She popped the top off the bin and set it aside. "Christmas at Rockefeller Center! I love this CD!" The collection of Christmas classics was supposedly made up of songs played at the ice skating rink at the famous New York landmark. To a young girl, the combination of songs and location were magic. When she was eight or nine, Santa surprised her with a pair of skates. She tied the laces together and put them over her shoulder, one skate in front and the other behind. Just like the girl on the back of the CD.

"Why don't you hang on to that, Aubrey?"

"Really?" She was nine again.

They shared a long, loving look. "Okay," Claire said, "let's see what else is in here. Hmmm. What's this?" Claire withdrew a large square box that had once held a pair of Randall's cowboy boots. "Ah. Our first Nativity set."

Aubrey had not seen that set since she was a very little girl. Randall bought it at Kmart for Claire's first Christmas gift. The figures were larger than most and made of hard plastic. Aubrey took the baby Jesus from the box—He was molded into the little manger—and held Him tenderly. Once the Porters decided they weren't as religious as their parents thought they were, Randall bought an expensive imported set that Claire put on the mantel every year just for show. Aubrey never touched it. Now she put the Kmart Jesus back in the box and set it aside.

Claire pulled out a bundle of used Christmas wrap with something inside it.

Aubrey recognized the technique and remembered the conversation her parents had every Christmas morning. Aubrey would tear open a present and Claire would pick up the wrapping paper, fold it, and set it aside. Randall would say, "Why do you do that? You have rolls and rolls of paper and you buy more every year."

"It's perfectly good paper, even if it never goes around another present."

Even until summer some years, Christmas wrap would turn up anywhere when something needed to be packed or decorated. The bundle Claire was holding in a hot garage on a warm Texas evening was protected by paper last used to wrap a present from who knows how long ago.

Claire let out a squeal. She recognized the object long before it was clear of the wrapper.

Aubrey watched intently. Her mother rotated and shifted the item as she freed it from the red and green paper. A flash of gold was followed by a pair of bare feet. Then came wings, and finally, a trumpet and a halo. "Our angel! When's the last time that sat on our tree?" Aubrey asked.

"I don't know," Claire said. "It's been . . . well, it's been a few years, at least. Since I lost the bin, I suppose." The angel stood nearly a foot tall. It wore a flowing gold robe and had matching golden wings. Its shiny ceramic face looked upward as it blew into a gold trumpet. Somehow, Aubrey remembered that it was handmade in Germany. She opened her mouth to ask about it, but stopped when she saw the hardness that had taken over her mother's face. "Well. He's not getting this," Claire said.

Aubrey felt Christmas slink back into its resting place. She stood and held out a hand to help her mother up from the floor. "Mystery solved. I've got some things to do before I go to bed. Do you need me for anything else?"

"No, I don't think so. Is something wrong?"

"Uh-uh." Aubrey shook her head. "I just have stuff to do."

"Go on, then, sweetie. I'm just going to put this back in the house with the rest of the decorations." She plucked the CD out of the top of the bin. "Don't forget this."

"Thanks." She looked at the girl with the little skates and the big smile. "Good night, Mom."

126 Days to Christmas

The difference between a lie and the truth came down to pure chance. If two phone calls had come in reverse order, Aubrey wouldn't have had to mislead her father. She considered this as they spoke.

"Tell me more about this job," he said.

"Well, it's an entry-level photographer position, like I said. It should be a good gateway into the business, even if I don't stay long." She measured her words carefully, skirting the lie like the attorney she'd never wanted to be. "There's a lot of shuffling around in the fashion and photography industries. Who knows, I might get there and take a different job right away."

"Sounds a little squishy to me. New York City is a big move for someone playing it by ear."

"I'll be fine, Dad. I know what I'm doing."

"Of course you do. I didn't mean to say otherwise. I'm just being a dad."

Really? You're being a dad now? "You mentioned something about lunch tomorrow. I'm not sure I can make it."

"Of course you can make it. Meet me downtown at Stone's. You can park in the garage. They validate."

She knew it was easier to accept than fight. "What time?"

"12:20. If I'm not there yet, just tell them you're waiting for me and they'll take you to my table."

"Okay. See you tomorrow, then." She pretended not to hear him say something else as she touched the End Call button on her iPhone for the second time in half an hour.

The other call was from the fashion photography company Aubrey's friend had introduced her to. Apparently, the person who said that she was "99.9 percent" sure they had a place for her no longer had a place of her own with the company. "We're very sorry that Gwen led you on. She meant well and had no way of knowing that we were about to restructure. Not only are we not hiring right now, we just let twenty percent of our staff go. Good luck to you, though."

And that was that.

She had no job and no prospects. Claire would love to have her stay at home, but that was simply not an option. Randall would love to help her find a "real" job. That wouldn't work either. Discouragement began to set in, but she fought it off. She opened her MacBook and said, "I'll just have to find a job." She took a deep breath. "Before lunch tomorrow."

It turned out to be easier than she imagined. A quick Google search turned up more than twenty photography firms in New York City, and a few clicks led her to an electronic job board. She posted her resume and uploaded her portfolio. She had four responses by dinnertime. By midmorning the next day, she had three phone interviews that resulted in two firm offers.

It's amazing how easy it is to get a job with a photography studio in New York City. Easy, that is, if you're willing to work as an unpaid intern.

❦

There is always something interesting to see in downtown Dallas. So, of course, Aubrey took her Nikon with her to lunch. She had a nice conversation with a state trooper after she stopped on an overpass to take her own version of Adams's freeway photo. After he let her go with a stern warning, she followed the highway until it ended on Main Street. By the time she pulled into the parking garage, she'd taken over a hundred shots, including a fresh set of Dealey Plaza.

She had several collections of that park taken at different times of year and in different lighting conditions. She, like nearly every photographer visiting Dallas, was drawn to the site because of its historical significance. She took so many pictures, though, because she found the place beautiful. Something was always casting an interesting shadow or reflecting a unique color. One of her favorite projects included bright, happy pictures interwoven with black and white images taken the day JFK was assassinated.

As she sat at a table waiting for her father to arrive, she considered how one place could be an accomplice in acts of both wonder and horror. The building she was sitting in, for instance, was the site of a Mafia hit during the '20s. Now it housed a ballroom in such demand that wedding planners booked it years in advance knowing that one of their clients would pay dearly to use it. Death and matrimony. The meeting she was about to have with Randall fell somewhere around the two on the what-Aubrey-would-like-to-be-doing scale.

He walked right past the hostess who turned on her heel to greet him as he breezed by. "Afternoon, Denise," he said without pausing or turning. "You're here," he said to Aubrey as he slid into his chair. "I thought you might give up on me."

"C'mon, Dad. We know how it works. On time for us is early for you. You aren't late until we've been waiting half an hour." She looked at her phone. 12:40. "You're exactly on time."

He grinned and picked up a menu. "I don't even know why I look at this. I have the thing memorized. I can even tell what most of my lunch guests are going to order before they do."

"What am I going to get, Dad?"

"That's an easy one. I know exactly what you'll order, but if I say it out loud, you're likely to suffer through something else just to prove me wrong." He took a pen and a business card out of his jacket pocket. "I'm writing your exact order down."

Aubrey watched the man she grew up with play with his little girl. She had come into the restaurant wanting—needing, maybe—to resent him. She wanted to blame him for divorcing her mother. She had to hold somebody accountable. He wasn't making it easy. He finished writing and put the card down on the table.

"No peeking," he said as he looked around. "Service is usually excellent here. I wonder where our waitress is." His eyes settled back on Aubrey, and he looked like he was about to say something when his attention shifted to his jacket. He took out his phone and scowled at it. "I've got to return this call, Aubrey. It'll only take a minute. Order whatever you want and get me the Cobb salad. I'll be right back." It was easier to resent Randall Porter, Attorney-at-Law, while watching him walk away with a cell phone to his ear.

She looked over the menu, trying to imagine what her father wrote on the card. If she ordered something unusual and didn't enjoy it, Randall would win. If she got something she often ate and he guessed right, he would win. The waitress came over. "Hi there, I'm Stephanie. Do you need another minute?"

Aubrey smiled as she determined how she would get the best of her father. "No, we're ready." She gestured across the table. "He will have the Cobb salad. And I will have the Cobb salad, as well, but without the bacon." *Guess that, old man!*

Randall came back faster than she'd expected, and she just knew he would announce that lunch was over or had to be cut short. But he said nothing about the phone call and didn't seem to be in any real hurry. "How's your mother holding up?"

"She's okay. Why do you ask?"

His eyes narrowed just enough to squeeze a wrinkle between them. "She's my ex, not my enemy. I knew it would be hard on her. On both of you. It was a really tough decision."

"Why did you do it, then?" This was not the conversation Aubrey wanted to have over lunch, but the question just popped out.

"Because it was time." He looked past his daughter and into the space above and behind her. "We just knew. We were tired, exhausted. I think we'd have lasted longer if we had fought more, but that wasn't Claire's way. She just absorbed everything until she was hard and cold. We couldn't stand to be in the same room." He looked at Aubrey again. "That's all there is to it. I bet your mother said just about the same thing."

"Just about."

"Hey, isn't that your friend Jake?" he pointed toward the door.

She turned around and stared for a second. "No. Not even close." She looked back at her father. "Way to change the subject," she said with more than a little relief.

"I'm sorry. Did you have another question?"

"No. Thanks for being so straight with me. People get divorced."

The salads arrived and Randall nodded as Aubrey took a smug first bite. "Very clever. But not clever enough." He gestured toward the card.

Aubrey picked it up and salad almost fell out of her mouth. *Cobb salad. No bacon.* "How in the world did you do that?!"

"I just know my little girl. Plus, I'm a little psychic." It was his turn to be smug. "So, you must be getting excited for the big move. It's just a few weeks, right?"

"Three weeks. It's moving fast. I haven't even found an apartment yet."

"Where is your office?"

Aubrey stepped back into the minefield of incomplete stories and just-over-half-truths. "It's on Madison Avenue near the flatiron district."

"That's a pricey neighborhood, I'll bet."

"Too expensive for me. I'll be spending some quality time on the subway."

"How much are they paying?"

"Not much to start." *Well, at least that's true.* "It's just an entry-level job."

"Aubrey, you're pretty talented and a hard worker. Make your mark and you should be all right."

"I hope so. It's starting to get a little scary."

"Being scared is good for you. Just don't let your boss see it."

They finished eating and Randall signaled for the check. Stephanie rushed over and said, "How did it go?"

"How did what go?" Aubrey asked.

Randall smiled. "You got me. During my pretend phone call, I asked Stephanie what you ordered. Then I switched cards while you were looking the other way."

"Cheater!"

"Gullible!"

A line came automatically to Aubrey's mind and almost out of her mouth. She'd said it thousands of times since she was a toddler. It was the go-to phrase before she let it change the expression on her face. *I'm telling Mom.*

104 Days to Christmas

*A*s the city grew to fill the windshield of the cab, Aubrey wished for a moment that her mother had asked one more time.

"Are you sure you don't want some help moving in, Aubrey?"

"No, Mom. I'll be fine."

It had been a lot easier to be confident when home was her parents' guest room and New York City was a twenty-by-thirty print on the wall. The mixture of feelings began to tilt from excitement toward apprehension as she heaved her third suitcase onto a luggage cart inside the entrance of DFW airport. The two emotions merged into a single, adrenaline-pumping anxiousness when she got off the plane at JFK. She was a pounding heart wrapped in a Dallas Cowboys sweatshirt by the time the Midtown Tunnel choked out the sun and replaced it with dirty orange lights.

The driver had rolled the windows partway down when he got on the expressway. Aubrey wasn't sure whether he meant to let the Indian Summer air in or the taxi smell out. It didn't matter now because the oily dustiness of the tunnel chased away all of the distant city scents Aubrey had enjoyed along the way. When the car emerged in Manhattan, the echoes of the Midtown Tunnel escaped into the shallow canyons between buildings. As the buildings got taller and the traffic denser, a nutty smell—*chestnuts?*—mixed with the exhaust of cars and busses. Aubrey took it all in as she got her first full taste of New York City.

The cab turned onto a narrow street. "You are very lucky today," the driver said with a heavy accent.

"Really?"

"Yes. That is 3440, yes? Your address?"

She mentally filled in the spots where white paint had flaked away from the house number. "Yeah. It looks like it."

His smile filled the rearview mirror. "See. We have parking spot right in front of building!" He pulled forward into the space, rolling two tires up onto the sidewalk right at the foot of the stairs leading to the ancient brownstone that would be Aubrey's new home.

By the time she finished struggling free of the seat belt and got out of the car, the driver was dropping the last suitcase onto the concrete and closing the trunk. "Thank you," Aubrey said as she handed over the fare and a generous tip.

"Oh. Thank you, miss. Enjoy the city."

Aubrey dragged the suitcases up the stairs one at a time and set them in the small lobby. She blessed her luck that the apartment was not on the second or third floor, as she fished an envelope out of her purse. In the envelope were two keys, a copy of her lease, and a business card. The first key barely went into the lock and would not turn. She held her breath as she tried the other key. It was stiff, but after a little hopeful wiggling, the lock turned and she was home.

Aubrey knew when she first saw them that the pictures the broker sent were taken with a wide-angle lens. Still, the compactness of the studio apartment surprised her. Two of them would have fit in the guest room she just came from. The "two HUGE closets" only counted as two because the opening was just big enough to accommodate two narrow sets of folding doors. They also represented the only storage in the apartment except for three small cabinets in the "kitchen." By the time she added the double bed, dresser and dining table/computer desk she still needed to buy, there would barely be room to move around.

She reviewed her math and felt better about her decision. In Brooklyn, she could have rented a similar apartment for less money or a larger place for the same amount. But then she would have had to commute farther and would not be able to put a Manhattan address on her resume.

The juggling act with her bank accounts was going to be tricky no matter what. She would pay rent out of her savings, and, if necessary, living expenses out of the account Randall set up. Using a few hundred dollars a month would probably even make him feel like he was contributing—without causing him to wonder about her general financial situation. She had a six-month lease and decided she could keep up the charade for three or four of those, at most. After that, she'd have to admit defeat and either leave or accept more help from her dad.

She puffed into the air mattress that would be her bed until she could have a real one delivered. Then she lay down on it and stared up with her photographer's eye at a water stain shaped roughly like a pine tree. *I will not fail.*

93 Days to Christmas

When Aubrey was sixteen, her parents took her to New York as a birthday present. She was just beginning to get serious about photography and the city is one of the best places in the world to see and take pictures. It was early November and Aubrey remembered being disappointed that none of the streets or stores were decorated for Christmas. "We'll come back for Christmas one day," Randall said.

They never did.

New York was not the only big city Aubrey had visited. She spent a lot of time in Dallas, had been to Chicago and San Francisco and even Washington, DC. But no other place was like New York City.

And visiting New York City was nothing like living there.

During the week and a half between her arrival and her first day of work, Aubrey explored as much of the city as she could. She was a tourist for the first three or four days and then became comfortable enough with her neighborhood to consider herself a new resident. By the beginning of the second week, she found herself avoiding Times Square because the tourists slow things down and get in the way.

Instead of crowding her apartment, her new furniture actually made it look bigger. She bought a twin bed with drawers in the base and a small five-drawer dresser. A square bar-height table with two stools separated the "bedroom" from the "dining room." She filled her three suitcases with framed photographs she wasn't going to hang and crammed them into the tiny storage locker in the basement. There simply wasn't enough empty wall space to tastefully display all the pictures she'd brought.

The night before her first day of work, she stood in front of her bathroom mirror and brushed her teeth. She angled the mirror so she could see the reverse version of her new favorite portrait behind her. One thing about New York she was really going to like: the ability to carry a thumb drive into one of several shops and come out with a photo printed any size on whatever kind of paper or canvas she liked. This one was of the street vendor who had fixed her a hot dog the day before. The cart's umbrella shaded one side of his weatherworn face. When she first reviewed in on the camera's display, it appeared unremarkable. Later, she cropped it and converted it to black and white. The man now looked like two people with a single face.

Like Aubrey.

Like Randall and Claire.

Like New York City.

⁓⊚

It was the third time Aubrey had been in the building on Madison Avenue. Today was special because she was doing more than admiring the open three-story lobby and giant photographs suspended at different heights by almost invisible wires. She sat on a beautiful but uncomfortable designer bench until a few minutes before eight.

Then, just as she imagined and precisely as she'd agreed on the morning of the Tuesday after Labor Day, she stood up, smoothed her skirt, and walked over to the receptionist.

"May I help you?" The woman was about Aubrey's age and obviously a native of the city.

"Yes. I work here. I mean, I start here today."

"What's your name?"

"Aubrey Porter."

The receptionist, who had been using a computer when Aubrey walked up, turned her attention to a clipboard holding several sheets of paper. She leafed through them while saying, "Portah . . . Portah . . . Portah . . . there you are. Intern. Lucky you." She half-smiled. "Go up to the third floor and through the double doors. Tyrone will take it from there." She pointed directly above her head. "You can wait for the elevator, but it's faster just to take the lobby stairs. They only go up to three."

"Thanks." She started to walk away and then turned. "What's your name?"

"Katherine. Welcome to Flare . . ." she looked at the clipboard, ". . . Aubrey."

"Thanks." She climbed the open stairs. As she turned the corner on the last landing, she saw a large ebony man behind a large ebony desk watching her through the glass double doors. "Are you Tyrone?" she asked as the door closed behind her.

His face was slack; his eyes gave no clue as to what he was thinking or what his mood might be. He turned his head slightly toward the bustling cubicle farm behind him. His head moved, but his eyes stayed fixed on Aubrey. "Fresh meat!" he called out. "Aubrey Porter." He looked at his computer screen. "New intern. Let's get you started."

86 Days to Christmas

It wasn't long before Aubrey understood why it was so easy to get an intern position. A guy named Forrest started the same day she did and was fired the following Monday because he came in ten minutes late without calling. Interns were the lowest of the low, and, ironically, the people who treated them the worst were the ones who graduated from intern to paid employee.

No task was too trivial or unpleasant to dump on Aubrey or one of the other three Flare interns. Her only ally was Tyrone. After he pushed her hard the first few days, she realized part of his job was to cull the intern herd. On her one-week anniversary, he said,

"You might last here a while longer, Porter." His words helped her make it through a particularly nasty day.

One of the photographers called her into the tiny studio permanently set up for taking pictures of small items. "Porter, I need to run some errands," she said without looking at Aubrey. "Everything is set up. I just need you to put each of these watches on that velvet cushion and take twelve pictures." She pushed on the round platform under the cushion and showed how it rotated. "Take one straight on, one turned to one o'clock, another at two o'clock, et cetera. Got it?"

"Yes, ma'am."

"Do not move the camera. Do not adjust the lights. Do not touch the shutter button; use this remote. Don't worry about running out of memory; the camera is connected directly to the computer." She waved at the Mac Pro next to the tripod. "I'll be back in an hour."

"Yes, ma'am." Aubrey looked at the stack of watch boxes. It looked like there were only seven or eight. "Just these right here?"

"These plus everything in those cartons. I'm not sure how many there are. A lot."

"Okay. Thanks."

"Seriously, Porter? You're thanking me for making you do my work? Where are you from?"

"Dallas."

The photographer rolled her heavily mascaraed eyes. "That explains it. Texas. See you in an hour."

In the week Aubrey had been at Flare New York Photography, she'd never been asked to do anything involving an actual camera. This assignment was just one step up from nothing, but it would result in real pictures. She looked at the setup and the camera. She pressed the button on the remote and heard the satisfying click of a high-end shutter. The image in the on-camera display looked good, so Aubrey rotated the turntable slightly and took another one. And another. After twelve pictures, she carefully removed the watch from the pillow and put it back in its box. Then she replaced it with the next one in line.

When she finished with the watches on the table, she opened the first carton on the floor. It was divided with strips of cardboard into sixteen compartments. In each compartment, she found a stack of five watch boxes. "Eighty watches," she said to herself as she counted the cartons. "Five cartons. Great. I get to shoot four hundred watches." *I didn't know there were that many different watches out there.*

An hour and a half later, the photographer swooshed into the studio. "Not finished?"

"It'll be a while. There are four hundred. I'm about . . ." Aubrey surveyed the boxes, ". . . a third of the way through."

"I suppose I should take over, now that I'm back."

Aubrey stepped away from the table. "Okay, if you want, but I'm happy to finish this for you."

"Right answer, Intern. You survived another day." She turned on her heel. "By the way, you need to finish before you leave for the day. Those watches go back to the client first thing in the morning."

Aubrey continued taking pictures and developed a rhythm that let her take all twelve pictures of each watch in about a minute. At five o'clock, the photographer came back and said, "About done?"

"Just about."

"Let's see how you did." She sat on the old piano stool in front of the computer and clicked the mouse. She scowled, pushed the mouse frantically around the desk, and clicked some more.

"You idiot! You never set up the connection between the camera and the computer!"

"I didn't know . . . you said it was connected."

"I most certainly did not. I gave you clear instructions. You either ignored me or weren't paying attention. Everything you did was wasted."

"I'm—"

"Fired. That's what you are. You are fired."

"Wait. I'll take them all again. I'll stay as late as I need to. Please let me." Aubrey knew it was a combination of her mother and father speaking through her. Randall never gave up. Claire always deferred and apologized.

"Fine. Take them all again. And then you're fired."

"You can't fire her, Tabitha. Only I can do that." Tyrone had arrived in the doorway during the tense conversation.

"Whatever. She screwed up. We've fired *real* employees for less."

After Tabitha left, Tyrone asked, "Did you screw up or did Tabitha not start you off right?"

He'd heard the whole conversation. "Either way, I should have known everything about what I was doing."

"I want to know. Was it you or Tabitha?"

"It was my responsibility."

Tyrone smiled, his goatee stretching wide while getting shorter. "You've got some work to do." He looked at his watch. "Do. Not. Walk. Home." He took a twenty from his wallet. "Take a cab. I'll tell security you'll be here a while. Just check out when you leave."

"What about Tabitha? Will she be okay? I mean, will we be okay?"

"First, never call her Tabitha. It's Tab. She hates it when people use her full name. That's why I do it." His smile got impossibly bigger. "Get these pictures reshot and she'll be fine." He headed for the door.

"Wait. Can you show me how to connect the camera to the computer?"

"Nope. No idea. You'll figure it out."

After fumbling around an unfamiliar interface, Aubrey made the connection and took a few test shots. Aubrey noticed some shadows she didn't quite like so she adjusted the lights and tweaked the exposure. *Tabitha's gone. It's my project now.* Then she spent the night taking pictures of watches.

71 Days to Christmas

*A*fter that night, Tyrone began filtering the tasks assigned to Aubrey. It was as though she'd cleared some invisible hurdle. One day, anyone could command her to do anything. The next, she would either get a task straight from Tyrone or her coworkers would say something like, "Tyrone wants you to format these flash cards for me." Aubrey had graduated from ultra-temporary-disposable intern to work-her-to-death-while-we-still-have-her intern. As she walked home after another long day, she wondered if she would ever move from Porter, the intern, to Aubrey, the future colleague. She wondered if she wanted to.

Living in New York City had, up until now, been an adventure. A frustrating, terrifying, sleep-deprived adventure, but an adventure nonetheless. She ate, shopped, and moved around the city like a native. Being a New Yorker in training was the most enjoyable part of her new life. She even managed to push thoughts about money into the back of her mind—until she got the email.

Balance alert. Your checking account ending in 6433 has fallen below your alert preference setting of $300. Deposit or transfer funds to avoid overdraft charges.

Aubrey had been using what was left in her checking account to outfit her apartment and buy food. Now, she was going to have to dip into her savings account for November's rent. Her plan to use Randall's graduation gift to pay for her other expenses was less attractive now that she was going to have to do it.

She sat at the table, her mouse in one hand and a fork in the other. The fork scraped the last grains of rice from a white cardboard container. The mouse led her to the bank web site where she transferred enough money to cover the rent.

She slowly took the five steps from the table to the kitchen and threw away the Chinese container. Then she opened the top drawer and pulled out an envelope with her father's handwriting on it. She took out the ATM card and put it on the counter. She put it all back.

54 Days to Christmas

*C*laire and Aubrey talked on the phone nearly every day for the first month after the move. Aubrey told herself it was so her mom wouldn't worry, but not so secretly she was glad to hear a friendly voice. They chatted about nothing and everything. Only the aftermath of the divorce was off limits by unspoken mutual agreement.

Claire was working in, of all places, a law office. She certainly didn't need the money, but she sure needed to be busy. Randall thought it was hilarious that the woman who was set for life because her ex-husband clawed his way to the top of the law profession was now "volunteering," as he said, at the bottom of the ladder.

By the end of September, the phone calls had become shorter and farther apart, but whenever Aubrey's iPhone rang, she knew it was most likely her mother.

By October, they were down to their scheduled weekend telephone visit and the occasional "just thinking about you" call.

On the first of November, Claire called for what Aubrey thought was one of those spur of the moment chats.

"How are you, dear?"

"I'm great. How 'bout you? How's work?"

"I was just going to ask you that. You first."

"Same old, same old. I'm still busy, but there is a lot more ladder above me than below."

"You'll get there. You're so talented. It's just a matter of time before they see."

"I hope so. Okay, so your turn. How is the world's oldest law clerk?"

"I am not the oldest. There's a lady I deal with in Houston who is six months older than I am. She's been clerking for ten years. So there."

"Pardon me," Aubrey said, laughing.

"It's actually been kind of fun lately. I have a way of looking at things that the other clerks don't. They get worked up when it gets hectic, but your mother stays cool as a cucumber."

"Maybe they're worked up because they're afraid of losing their jobs."

"Maybe so. But it doesn't help to get all rattled. In fact, some of the partners steer work to me because they know I'm . . ."

"Mature?"

"Seasoned."

"I hope to live long enough to reach your level of seasoning, Mom."

"Enough talk about my level of experience. I have news."

"Okay . . ."

"I'm coming to New York for a visit."

"When?" Aubrey knew Claire would want to come at some point, but she was still trying to adapt to the idea while sounding excited.

"Around Thanksgiving. Since you said you couldn't get away to come visit me . . . us . . . I thought I would come to you. You can still do Thanksgiving on your own, if you insist. I can come before or after."

"Mom, I know you don't understand the whole thing about me wanting to stay here over the holidays. It's just that I'm finally getting a life of my own, a real life, and I know being back there with all those memories would set me back. Next year, we can have a big family whatever."

"Count on it. That promise is the only reason I'm not worrying you to death about this year."

"I'm not trying to be a party pooper, Mom, but they told me at work to get ready to be busy at Christmastime. The paid . . . the *higher* paid people take a lot of time off and we *newbies* have to take up the slack."

"You still get weekends, don't you? That and one day is all we'll need. Even if you have to work some while I'm there, that's fine. I can find something to do on my own."

"I've got a small place. That okay?" *Or you could stay in a hotel . . .*

"That's wonderful. I'll get the real New York experience."

"What would you like to see or do while you're here? If you want to see one of the popular shows, I'd have to get tickets soon."

"A show would be nice. And we will shop. Really shop. I miss a lot about you, Aubrey, but some days, I miss my shopping buddy most of all."

Aubrey had been working so hard to absorb the thought of a visit she hadn't processed what it would mean for Claire to be coming right in the middle of New York City during Christmas season. "I miss that, too, Mom, and the stores will all be decorated for

Christmas. So will lots of the streets. And Rockefeller Center. We could go ice skating!"

Claire laughed. "That sounds wonderful. I'm glad to hear you so excited."

"It'll be fun, Mom. I'm looking forward to it."

"So am I. And I better let you go. We'll chat again on Sunday and start working out details."

"Okay, Mom. Bye."

When the phone rang just a minute after she hung up, Aubrey assumed her mother had forgotten something. She didn't even look to see who it was. "What's up, Mom? Your seasoned brain forget something?"

"So," Randall Porter said, "Your old dad can't call once in a while?"

She sat up straight. "Sorry, Dad. I just hung up with Mom and thought she was calling right back."

"I see. That's nice. How is she?"

"You'll have to ask her yourself, Dad. I'm not going there."

"Don't read so much into it. I was only asking. Making conversation."

"Sorry. What's up?"

"Just calling to check on you. I noticed you haven't used your graduation account yet. Are you eating?"

"I'm fine for now. Between my pay and what I put away during my last semester, I'm making ends meet."

"Let me help, Aubrey. You can't be really enjoying life in New York on that kind of money."

"You're already helping, Dad. Where did my savings come from in the first place? I didn't sock away a few grand by taking double shifts at the book store."

"We agreed I would pay list price for four years at a good school. If you could do it for less, the excess was yours. You did well. I considered it an investment, by the way, in a very talented young woman."

"Photographer."

"Photographer." He still seemed to choke on the word a little. Aubrey knew he still wished she'd done something he considered more serious.

"I'm fine, Dad, really. If I get in a bind, I will use the card. Really."

"Okay. Have you gotten a raise yet? You must be knocking their socks off by now."

"No raise, yet. I'm hoping for something before the end of the year."

"Maybe you'll get a nice Christmas bonus."

"Maybe." *I'll settle for a paying job cleaning lenses.*

"So . . . it looks like I'm going to be up your way in a few weeks."

"Really?"

"One of our biggest clients wants to bring us into some business he's got going in New York. I'd normally hand this off to one of the guys, but since he's so important and since it's New York, I thought I would take it."

"Are you sure you'll have time to socialize?"

"I'll make time. Since you aren't coming to Texas this Christmas, I reckon Texas will have to come to you."

"Sounds good. When are you coming?"

"Don't know exactly. Late this month or early next. Before Christmas week, for sure. These folks are gonna want to wrap up this deal in time to get to the Bahamas or Hawaii or wherever they're headed."

"That's the opposite of my work. It will be really busy for me."

"I wouldn't interfere with your work. We'll just be tourists together for a while. Maybe go to a couple museums or something. Just no opera."

"No opera. Got it."

"I miss you, Aubrey."

She took the phone from her ear and looked at it. Her father's expressionless face was in the center of a small box on the screen. The box was labeled "Randall." She held it flat in front of her mouth and said, "Me too."

"All right then. I'll let you know more about the trip. Talk to you later."

"Bye, Dad."

Aubrey navigated to the screen listing her father's phone number and details. She looked at the display name and felt guilty. She had put it in there after Claire told her about a particularly unpleasant conversation she'd had with her father.

She changed the label to "Dad."

27 Days to Christmas

The way Aubrey described her Thanksgiving plans to her parents led them to believe she was skipping the holiday altogether. She didn't want Claire, in particular, to try and reconstruct something the divorce had entirely destroyed. Whatever "the holidays" became would be entirely different than what it was when Aubrey was growing up.

Randall said he understood and wouldn't put any pressure on Aubrey to come home. She wondered if that was because he supported his daughter or if he was relieved not to have to deal with what was bound to generate some serious drama.

Claire was a tougher sell. Eventually, Aubrey had to just tell her, "Mom, you're not listening. We are not doing Thanksgiving this year. Christmas either. If you want to even talk to me on those days, you will let it go."

What she didn't tell her parents was she planned to make her own holiday memories. She was in the Big Apple, after all, and people came from all over the world to see and do what the city had to offer. She even considered this the adult Aubrey's First Christmas.

At nine o'clock on Thanksgiving, she dressed for the cold morning and put on her most comfortable sneakers. She stepped out onto the sidewalk and began walking. Every block was more crowded than the last, and by the time she made it to Sixth, there was hardly room to stand, let alone move. The crowd was a living, happy, content creature. It laughed with a thousand voices and smiled with a thousand very different faces.

She had the longest and most expensive lens she owned attached to her Nikon. The empty case and part of a small tripod stuck out of the top of her camera backpack. She'd successfully used the "excuse me, press photographer coming through" trick many times, but never in a city known for its attitude. She aimed for the opening between two strollers and pressed her way through with a smile and an apologetic wave. After a dozen "excuse me's," she was against the police barrier at the front of the crowd.

The noise of the gathered families, tourists, and a few locals echoed through the canyon, bouncing between buildings until being absorbed by a blanket of coats, hats, and mittens. The sound level stayed the same as they waited for the parade, but its nature changed. Aubrey began to hear band instruments and cheering mixed with the chatter of those around her. As the parade sounds got louder, the chatter got quieter, until the first float turned the corner from Forty-Second Street. It was still too far away to see clearly, but every head was turned toward it.

Aubrey had watched the parade a dozen times on television and thought she knew what to expect. There would be bands and balloons, floats and minor celebrities, shriners, and, eventually, Santa. What she didn't expect was the feeling of the thing. The reality of it. The sounds pushed against her. The closeness erased the perfection her memory and technology had created. Balloons were dirty and scarred with stitched repairs. Shoes were dull and costumes frayed at the edges. The zoomed-in image of Santa she saw through her viewfinder revealed a man in a crushed velvet suit that didn't quite fit. But he was smiling. Not wearing a smile, but really smiling. So was Aubrey.

After a lunch of leftovers, she video chatted with both of her parents and her grandparents. The calls were an hour apart. She visited with her father and his father for half an hour and then with Claire and her parents. It was like watching old home movies on her laptop. The tone was the same as every time she had been there in person. Randall moved in and out of the frame as he found other things to do. Claire entertained her parents while making Aubrey recite every detail of her life as a "New York Girl." She felt exactly the same as she had in third grade telling her grandparents about her recorder solo in the school holiday concert.

As she was getting ready to end the call with her mother, Claire said, "I miss you so much, Aubrey." She was beginning to cry.

"Me too, Mom. Me too." Aubrey's eyes got wet, but no tears escaped to her cheeks. "You'll be up here before you know it. We'll have a great time."

Claire blew her nose. "You better believe it, sister."

"Bye, Mom."

"Bye, sweetheart."

Aubrey clicked the conversation closed. With the green light of the camera off, she was free to cry on her own for a few minutes. She cried for her parents. She cried because she was alone in the biggest city. She cried because she didn't know if she was going to make it as a photographer. She cried because Santa didn't wave at her.

Then she stopped crying, declared Thanksgiving over, and went out for pizza.

21 Days to Christmas

"Porter, I want you and Jud to take some pictures tonight," Tyrone said.

"Tonight?" Aubrey wasn't against working in the evening, but two things confused her about the request. First, she was being told to take actual photographs. Second, she was supposed to do it after hours.

"Unless the tree lighting was moved to lunch time." He was trying not to smile.

"Seriously?! Rock Center?"

"Rock Center. We do this every year. It's cheaper to have our own library than buy someone else's stock. We even sell some of the good ones. You are going to take some good ones, aren't you, Porter?"

"Seriously? Rock Center? Yes, yes, yes. I will take some awesome pictures."

"We'll see. Jud is going along to help with the gear. Go see Tab and check out a camera, one of the Canon long lenses and whatever else you think you need."

"You are letting me take a company camera?"

"You'll be taking company pictures, won't you? I wouldn't want to bet on that crappy old thing you're hauling around."

Aubrey was too excited to let Tyrone's insult get to her. After nearly three months on the job, she was finally going to be a photographer. "Thanks, Tyrone. I appreciate it."

"And the intern indoctrination is complete," he said with a grin. "You are, once again, thanking Flare for working you to death. For no money. Whoever came up with the idea of interns should get some kinda prize."

He could tease all he wanted, but Aubrey knew what this assignment meant. Even if Flare didn't hire her, this assignment showed they had faith in her potential. It also meant she could ask for a glowing recommendation on company letterhead. She was a few hours and a hundred festive photos away from a real shot at being a professional New York photographer.

She and Jud Ricks, an intern in his first week on the job, walked out of the building at 6:30 with what Aubrey figured was about nine thousand dollars worth of photography equipment. They hailed a cab and climbed in the back. Aubrey carried the camera and lens herself. She wasn't about to let a new intern handle the gear. He could haul around the tripod and other accessories.

"Rockefeller Center," she said to the driver.

"It's a madhouse down there. You want I should drop you off a block over on Forty-Sixth? It'll be faster to walk a couple blocks than sit with me in traffic. Plus, my shift ends soon and I gotta get home."

"That's fine." The cab sped off and took a route Aubrey knew was taking them several blocks out of the way, but avoiding the worst of the traffic.

He stopped in the middle of Forty-Sixth Street and said, "This is as good as it gets."

Aubrey handed him a twenty and said, "Let's go, Jud."

They bailed out of the taxi just as the light changed and had to hustle to the sidewalk to avoid getting run over. Aubrey gestured to the left, but Jud Ricks was looking right and waving. "Yo! What are you doing up here?"

A pair of attractive young women emerged from the shadows between streetlights and walked quickly toward Jud and Aubrey. "We were shopping," the brunette said.

"Yeah, why are you here?" the blonde cocked her head.

"I'm supposed to help her take some pictures."

"Too bad. We're headed to Zach's now."

Jud looked at Aubrey. The straps for the camera and the huge lens crossed on her chest like a soldier's bandolier. Jud took off the backpack he wore and set it on the sidewalk. Annoyed New Yorkers stepped around the group, some muttering helpful suggestions about where they should go. "You got this," Jud said, "I'm going with my friends."

"What do you mean you're going with your friends? You're supposed to help me."

"You don't need me. Just put on the backpack and then sling the camera gear on. You're only a couple blocks away anyhow. You'll be fine."

"You know Tyrone will fire you for sure if you leave me."

"Great." He smiled at Blondie. "It was only a matter of time anyway. Now I can sleep in tomorrow." A wink. "I have a feeling I might be up a little late tonight."

Jud and the girls walked back the way Aubrey had just come in the cab. Only the brunette looked back with a look of mild concern or pity on her face. Aubrey stood shocked in the middle of the sidewalk with twenty or thirty pounds of photography equipment.

She looked around and saw she was right in front of a vacant storefront. "For Lease. Call Addison Properties. 555-1494." She picked up the backpack by one of its straps and stepped into the alcove in front of the whitewashed door. The tripod tipped out of the pack and clattered to the sidewalk, one of its legs extending a few inches. It lay there on the ground like an injured animal.

She bent down and pushed the leg back into place and latched it closed. She hunched over with her hands on her thighs, trying to figure out how in the world she was going to strap on all that gear and make it three or four long blocks in heavy foot traffic.

She didn't see the two men stop on the sidewalk in front of her. When she looked up, one of them was staring right at her. The other had his back to them both, his generous girth shielding his partner from view and turning the alcove into a very small, very dark crime scene.

"Give me the cameras." His eyes were wild and bloodshot, but his voice was somehow both calm and terrifying. Every grisly scene from every episode of CSI or Law and Order she'd ever watched flashed through her head. She took off the camera and lens and handed them to him. Anyone could have seen her hands shaking from three blocks away. The man picked up the backpack and pressed a strap into his partner's hand. "Now, sit down on the ground."

Aubrey sat down cross-legged and stared at the man's filthy Nike's. She stopped breathing and noticed the man's feet remained perfectly still. She closed her eyes tight and silently offered the first prayer she remembered in far too long. Finally, after what felt like hours, she looked up and saw a hand held out toward her, the fingers forming a gun. The man pressed his thumb against his index finger as if firing at Aubrey. "Bang."

The two thieves walked slowly away leaving Aubrey shaking on the ground. The robbery lasted less than a minute.

Once the shadow of the mammoth thug cleared the doorway, the lights on the street seemed to hit Aubrey like a spotlight. She continued to sit on the ground as the crowd bustled past, few looking at her at all and many deliberately not looking at what they must have thought was a vagrant begging for change.

She knew she should chase after the men or at least run in their general direction while shouting for a cop. But she didn't. After several more minutes, when she thought her rubbery legs would hold her, she stood up and walked toward the very small park near the corner. It only had three benches and someone was stretched out on one, asleep or otherwise unconscious. She sat in the only vacant wrought iron bench and tried to gather her thoughts. Her brain knew exactly what to do next, but her body was catching up, trying to flush the adrenaline that was still making her heart pound.

A man sat next to her. "You owe me fifty bucks."

Aubrey jumped up and prepared to run, but the calm smiling face looking up at her made her pause. "Sorry?"

He held up the five thousand dollar lens the thieves had taken just a few minutes before. "Fifty bucks. That's what I just paid for this."

She sat back down and took the lens. She held it where the streetlight would allow her to examine every inch of it, looking for a chip or scratch. Both caps were still on and it appeared to be fine. "How did you get this? Do you know those guys?"

"Just met them. A little sketchy, if you ask me."

"I don't understand. How did you . . . why did they give it to you?"

"I was walking right over there." He pointed across the street. "These two big rough guys stepped out of an alcove with camera gear and left behind a very upset girl. It was none of my business, but when they walked right to me, I had to do something."

He stopped and looked at Aubrey. She waited for a few seconds and said, "What? What did you say?"

"Oh. Yeah. I thought you'd never ask." He smiled at her with perfect teeth and brilliant blue eyes. "I figured they stole that stuff from you, and being the coward I am, I wasn't about to get my head cracked with a telephoto lens. So I just said, 'Nice camera. How much you want for it?' He looked at me a little funny and said, 'Five hundred.' All I had on me was fifty and I guessed he had no idea how much the lens was worth. Plus he was probably regretting stealing that beast anyway. Might as well hang a sign around his neck saying 'I just stole this.' Anyway, I said, 'All I have is a fifty. How about just that other lens thingy?' Then he just handed it over. I gave him the fifty and he kept on walking."

Aubrey's mouth was hanging open as she hugged the lens. Her chin was resting on the large black cap on the wide end. The blond knight in blue jeans and rimless glasses smiled again and said, "So, you owe me fifty bucks." She still couldn't speak. He continued. "Are you okay?"

"Yeah," she finally muttered. "Yeah. I think so. It's just catching up to me."

"What's your name?"

"Aubrey. And you?"

"Joel." He stuck out his hand.

Aubrey shook it. "Nice to meet you, Joel. And thank you."

"No problem. I wish I'd had more money on me. I could have rescued your whole kit."

"You would have done that?"

"Sure. I have a feeling it would be nice to have you owing me lots of money."

"What's that supposed to mean?"

He blushed. "Nothing. I don't know. Sometimes I just say things. Sorry."

Aubrey smiled. "Don't worry about it. I don't have fifty dollars on me right now, but I can get it for you. Right now I suppose I should go find a cop."

"You don't have to pay me back. I'll consider it my good deed for the day. For the month, really."

"No, no, I want to pay you." She pulled a dog-eared business card out of her front pocket. "Call this number and ask for Aubrey. We'll get together and I'll have your money."

"As long as we're going to get together, why don't you just take me to dinner? Then we'll call it even."

"Now, what do you mean by *that*?" Her eyes narrowed.

"Nothing," he blushed again. "I mean, it's New York. Dinner for two almost anywhere will hit fifty bucks. And I . . . I . . ."

"Just kidding. Relax."

"You are . . ." he paused and held her gaze. "You are *intriguing*."

"You have no idea." She stood up as a pair of police officers walked by. "Call me," she said as she walked away.

"Will do, intriguing Aubrey."

⌒◌

Instead of taking amazing pictures of the tree lighting ceremony at Rockefeller Center, Aubrey spent the next two hours in a hard chair next to a cluttered desk in the seventeenth precinct. It only took the detective ten minutes to take her statement; the rest of the time was spent waiting for her turn.

"Do you think you'll catch the guys?"

"Dunno. Depends on how smart they are. If they try to unload it soon to one of the usual places, we might get a match on the serial numbers. If they hold off a while and sell it on eBay or something, they'll probably get away with it."

"Awesome."

"Since it was too dark to get a good look at the guy, finding the gear is the only real chance we have at nabbing them."

"Is there anything else I need to do?"

"Not right now. If we come up with anything, we'll call you."

It was almost nine o'clock when Aubrey walked out of the building and over the two blocks to the subway. She told herself nobody would be in the office at Flare and she had no way to reach anyone until morning. She did not look forward to telling Tyrone she'd lost one of Tab's cameras. She did not even want to picture what it would be like to tell Tab.

Aubrey had never been afraid of the city. It had never given her a reason to be. She stayed out of the rough areas altogether and was careful to stay around lots of people. But now, as she rode the subway, carrying the expensive lens, she looked at everyone differently. Every glance her way was an assessment: *What is that thing worth? What else is she carrying that I can snatch?*

As she climbed out of the subway in her neighborhood, she stopped in a bodega and bought a large bottle of water. "I'd like that in a bag, please. Actually, could I get that double bagged? I have a long walk."

The clerk shot an odd look, but obliged. Aubrey stepped outside and carefully lowered the lens into the bags, testing them to make sure they would hold it securely. She opened the water and began drinking it. She felt better believing that anyone watching her would see a woman drinking water while walking home from the store with a few groceries.

She locked herself in her apartment and went to bed. Not to sleep, she regretted, but to bed.

20 Days to Christmas

Still on edge after the robbery, Aubrey noticed every glance her way, every rough looking character, and anything that seemed out of place. As she walked into Flare and past the front desk, she thought the receptionist looked at her differently than usual. She desperately wanted to turn around and go home. But where was home? The apartment in Chelsea? Dallas? Her childhood bedroom?

Her parents' voices took over. Two decades of upbringing led her up the stairs to "face the music." She "held her head high" as she strode toward Tyrone.

He didn't wait to hear the speech she'd been working on in her head since two o'clock in the morning.

"I already know. The cops came in looking for Jud so they could interview him." He shuffled through some papers and held one up. "And to get the serial numbers of the $8,945 dollars and sixty cents worth of equipment you lost."

"I wanted to tell you last night, but I had no way to reach you."

"Aubrey, I have fired 124 interns here. 125, actually, since I canned Jud this morning. Some are harder than others."

Aubrey braced herself and wondered if she should lower her head and plead for mercy. She didn't realize until that moment how much she didn't hate working at Flare. She held Tyrone's gaze and nodded.

He continued, "Firing you would be the hardest I can remember."

"Would be?"

"Would be . . ." he paused, ". . . if you hadn't already quit."

"I don't understand. I like working here. Why would I quit?"

"You'd quit so I don't have to fire you. So you can leave here with a reference letter instead of a black mark."

"Couldn't I just get another chance?" She took one herself and added, "It really wasn't my fault; I didn't do anything wrong." She handed over the double-bagged lens. "I managed to get the long lens back. That should count for something."

"I see it your way, Aubrey." He put the bag on his desk without looking inside. "If I didn't, you wouldn't have made it past Katherine downstairs. But Flare has a lot of written and unwritten rules about interns. There's no way one stays here after losing equipment, no matter how it happens."

Tyrone looked down at his desk for a moment and then back at Aubrey. The look on his face told her he was a friend trying to help, not a manager representing his cutthroat company. "Do I need to sign a resignation or anything?" Aubrey asked.

"No. You just told me in person. Do you have any personal stuff here?"

"Just a few things."

He nodded past him to the cube farm. "Go ahead. I'm supposed to escort you, but too many people around here enjoy watching the walk of shame. Be quick and then get on your way."

It took all of her strength to release the word "thanks" without crying. When she came back, she hung a green fabric grocery bag full of pictures, pens, and other things on the back of Tyrone's chair and gave him a long hug. He hugged back.

⌒っ

The only available bench in Madison Square Park had some unrecognizable grime on it, so Aubrey took an old magazine out of the green bag, spread it open, and sat. She began to inventory the things she took from her cubicle at Flare: two pictures from her award-winning college photo essay, the picture of her parents she took in the restaurant in Albuquerque, some photography magazines, a little "lady's emergency kit" as her mother called it, and some business cards she'd collected from Flare clients.

She put what she wanted to keep back in the bag and carried the rest to a nearby trash can. She was about to drop in a stack of her Flare business cards when she thought about Joel. *He's going to call the office. He may never find me.*

Rather than go straight back to her apartment, she decided to stay out and clear her head. She rode the subway to Central Park. As she emerged from underground on Fifty-Seventh Street, she could see bare tree limbs where the lines of buildings came to an end. It was a little too cold for the jacket she was wearing, but the sun was shining and she knew it would be nice by the pond.

One of the things she loved most about New York City was she could be alone in a sea of people. She could know she was part of the world. She could see others who she knew were experiencing the highs and lows of life. But they each moved in their own little circle. Back in Dallas, most people seemed to force themselves into a community. Make eye contact. Force a "howdy."

She was so deep in thought she didn't notice her phone vibrating until the caller was likely about to give up. She caught it at the last second. "Hullo?"

"Intriguing Aubrey?"

She smiled for the first time all day. "That's me. How did you get my number?"

"It wasn't easy. I called the number on your card. The receptionist told me you didn't work there anymore. I was afraid you'd given me an old card to get rid of me."

"But you didn't give up."

"I'm not a quitter. Well, usually. Sometimes I quit when I need a nap. Or stuff gets hard. But not this time. I went right down to that office and demanded to see the manager."

"Uh-huh."

"We got in a big argument—a fistfight, actually—and just before I took him out with a sleeper hold, the manager gave me your number."

"Well, that's a great story, Joel, but unless you are a ninja or some special forces guy, you wouldn't stand a chance against Tyrone."

"Tyrone. That is definitely the right name for that guy."

"What really happened?"

"Okay, I exaggerated a little. I did go down to Flare since it was like three blocks away from where I was when I called. Tyrone overheard me telling the receptionist about last night and he came over. He was nice—must like you a lot—took me upstairs, said he was breaking the rules big time, and pulled up your phone number on his computer. He told me to say 'hello,' by the way."

"Really? That doesn't sound like him."

"Well, he looked like he wanted to tell me to tell you 'hello.'"

"So, you found me. Now what. Dinner at the Four Seasons? I'm only a couple blocks away."

"Better. Meet me at Grand Central at . . . six. Okay?"

"Okay."

"I'll be inside by the main clock. You know where I'm talking about?"

"I think so. At the information desk."

"That's it. Six o'clock."

She never made it to the clock in the middle of Grand Central Terminal. Joel must have guessed the route she would take because he was standing next to the door to the Forty-Second-Street entrance.

"Hi," he said. As far as Aubrey could tell, he was wearing exactly the same outfit he had on when they first met almost twenty-four hours ago. But now, in the brightly lit entryway, she could see his jeans were Levi's, but his shirt was Armani.

"What's with the fancy shirt?"

"Oh, this old thing? I just pulled it out of the closet."

"Mmm-hmm."

He gestured and started to walk down the street and then stopped next to a newsstand. Aubrey stepped out of the foot traffic and stood facing him. "I'm sorry," he said.

"For what?"

"For not being more sensitive. As I gave my statement to the police this morning, I realized what a big deal last night must have been for you. You could have been hurt. You lost the camera. Then today you lost your job. So here comes some guy you just met and asks you out like nothing happened."

"It's okay. I'm glad to be out of the apartment."

"It's just that this isn't like me. I plan things. I'm deliberate, careful. I got ahead of myself and should have made sure you were okay; that this date is okay."

"Wait a minute, mister. This is a *date*?"

"See, that's why I'm here. You intrigue me."

"Let's see if you still feel that way after you see me eat. Where to, Joel? And keep in mind we're on a fifty-dollar budget."

"Won't be a problem." He stepped back into the pedestrian river and led Aubrey down the street. "All I know about you is that you are pretty, sassy, and good at getting robbed. And you used to work at Flare New York Photography."

"That's four things. I only know two about you. You walk the streets of New York in the evenings and like to buy stolen merchandise. Oh, and you wear two-hundred-dollar shirts with thirty-dollar jeans. So you still owe me one."

"Okay . . . I moved here from California."

"Texas."

"I'm nearsighted with an astigmatism."

"Twenty twenty."

"Six feet tall, a hundred seventy-five pounds."

"Five four, none of your business."

"Pizza."

"Pizza."

He stopped at the corner and gestured across the street. "I hope they held our table."

By the time Aubrey's brain had read and processed the words of the sign, her stomach was already gurgling in anticipation. *Anna's Pizza*. "Awesome."

They crossed the street and Joel held the door open for Aubrey. The narrow restaurant had a row of seats in front of a shallow counter facing out the window, booths along one wall, and a few tables farther back. The preparation area and ovens were along the other long wall. A dozen pizzas sat behind a glass partition waiting to be handed to hungry New Yorkers one slice at a time. "What kind do you like?" Joel asked.

"I always get pepperoni and extra cheese when I'm checking out a new place. If they can't get that right, there's no point in coming back."

"Good call. Now watch this." He rang the bell next to the "ring here for service" sign.

A man in his sixties walked over and looked at Aubrey while he said to Joel, "What can I get you?"

"I'd like a pepperoni pizza with extra cheese."

"Sorry, we only sell by the slice."

"All right, I'll have twelve slices. Four for here and eight to go." The man just stood there. Joel turned to Aubrey. "What do you think of their policy?"

"It's unusual and a little quaint."

"Is it intriguing?"

"I guess so," Aubrey answered. The pizza man smiled as he and Joel exchanged glances before he went to make pizza. She continued, "What was that all about?"

"Francis and I have a minor difference of opinion about the slices-only thing. You may have just won me over to his side."

"Interesting."

"What's interesting?"

"That he cares what you think. On the other hand, you did just buy a whole pizza for two people."

"Correction," Joel laughed. "*You* just bought a whole pizza. I will have delicious cold pizza for breakfast for the next three days."

Joel led Aubrey to the last booth. It had a "reserved" sign on it, which Joel pushed aside. "You weren't kidding," Aubrey laughed. "Just how often do you eat here?"

He answered, but she wasn't listening. She was capturing the scents and sights coming from all directions. They were close enough to the kitchen to smell raw garlic and fresh tomato sauce. They were close enough to the ovens to smell warm crust and bubbling cheese. She looked past him at the wall. It was covered with an eclectic mix of New York memorabilia: a few signed pictures of famous people, a Yankees pennant, a hundred postcards, and a dozen posters. Right over Joel's shoulder was a framed vinyl record from the seventies. *Imagine* by John Lennon. Joel started talking again after a short pause. "Hello, anybody home?"

"I'm sorry. I wasn't paying attention. Curse of the photographer. This place is too awesome."

"Apology and compliment both accepted."

While they waited for their pizza, the pair continued getting to know one another, without revealing too much. Aubrey talked about college and the internship, but not the divorce. Joel talked about growing up in California and how different New York was.

Aubrey had never before become so comfortable with someone so quickly. She wasn't even self-conscious as she shoved a folded piece of pepperoni pizza into her mouth as far as it would go.

Francis came over as they were finishing up their pizza. "How was it?"

Aubrey finished chewing the last of her crust and answered, "Good. No, more like really, really good."

He smiled and turned to Joel. "How 'bout you, partner?"

"Tremendous, as usual. Next time I'll talk Miss Aubrey here into trying Anna's special."

"She'll love it." He put a hand on Aubrey's shoulder. "You'll love it."

"I can't wait to try it."

Aubrey and Joel left Anna's, stepping out of the warm restaurant and into a brisk early December night. This time, Aubrey was wearing the right coat and she buttoned it up as they walked. "Where now?"

"Well, if you're up for a walk, I thought we would finish your assignment."

"What?"

"Your assignment. Pictures of Rockefeller Center."

"I'm pretty sure that gig died when they fired me."

"So you didn't want to take those pictures? I thought you said you were excited for the chance."

"I was but . . . look, I don't even have my camera."

Joel slid his North Face daypack off his shoulder and took out a Canon digital SLR camera. "I just got this at B&H. Thought you might show me how to use it."

Aubrey took the camera and stepped under a streetlight. "This just came out. How long have you had it?"

"Not very long."

She raised her eyebrows.

"Okay, okay. I bought it this afternoon, but I've been meaning to get a good camera. Today just seemed like a good day to do it since I was going to be out with a professional photographer."

"Now *you're* the intriguing one. Levi's, Armani, pizza and thousand-dollar impulse buys. Are you a drug dealer?"

"Not any more," he deadpanned. "Now I'm a contract assassin."

"Mmm-hmm. I almost believe you after the way you took out that pizza."

"So, what do you say? Shall we go take some pictures of a giant Christmas tree?"

When they got to the plaza, Aubrey sat Joel down on a concrete bench and explained the camera's controls. She helped him take a couple of pictures and review them on the camera's display. Then she stood up and asked, "What looks interesting enough to capture forever?"

Joel took a few steps until he could get a good shot of the tree. He moved left and then a little right and then pressed the shutter.

They looked at the picture together and Aubrey said, "Very nice. Now my turn." She walked along the reflecting pool and stepped up on its ledge. Angels formed from white wire lined the long pool. She adjusted the camera, held it above her head next to an angel's hand, and took a picture. She looked at it on screen, made some adjustments, and took another shot. She was smiling when she returned to Joel's side.

He studied the image Aubrey had just created. White wire fingers held the end of a white wire trumpet against white wire lips. The tree and buildings served as an out-of-focus background. "Wow," he said.

"Anybody can work a camera these days. Most people can take pretty good pictures—like yours. But you have to see things differently to take powerful photographs." She paused. "Listen to me. I'm bragging. I don't mean to. I just love to see things differently."

"I understand. Let me have another try." He took a picture of a store window that held a reflection of the tree. It seemed to float in front of two mannequins dressed for winter.

"Now, let's see your phone."

"Why?"

"Come on, I want to show you something."

He took out his phone and started to hand it to her. "No," she said, "you hold on to it. Bring up the Flickr photo sharing site."

"I'm not following."

"That's okay. Now type 'Rockefeller Center Christmas tree' in the search bar. Now what do you see?"

He laughed. "About fifty pictures exactly like the first one I took."

"Do you see any like the other one you took or the one I took?"

He scrolled through a few pages of images. "Nope."

"That's because we saw things differently. All these people are in the same place seeing the same things. A lot of us are taking pictures. Every picture captures something important. But not every picture is *art*."

They took turns taking many more pictures. Aubrey explained light and shadow, focal length, aperture and shutter speed. Joel absorbed it all and was a quick study. After an hour of wandering around the plaza, they went into the subway together. "You want me to walk you home?" Joel asked.

"No, I'm okay."

"You don't want me to know where you live."

"A girl's got to be careful nowadays. I don't even know your last name."

"Miller. Joel Miller."

"Nice to meet you, Joel Miller." She shook his hand and let him hold on to it for a second before pulling it back. "Thanks to Tyrone, you have my mobile number."

"And you still owe me twenty-five bucks worth of food. Don't worry, I'll call."

They rode a number seven train west to Times Square, where Joel changed to an uptown train and Aubrey went home to Chelsea. As she climbed the steps to her apartment, she realized she'd not thought once about the robbery or her job while she was taking pictures with Joel.

19 Days to Christmas

The gentle sound of a babbling brook jarred Aubrey awake. She reached for her phone to tell the alarm clock app to leave her alone for nine minutes. As she selected "snooze" from the menu, she became alert enough to realize she could snooze until noon if she wanted. The predawn hike to Flare was not on the agenda for the day. She had no agenda.

She listened to the brownstone wake up and start its day. Steam burbled through radiators as her neighbors tried to warm their apartments for the morning. Her ceiling creaked and bumped as the couple upstairs finished breakfast.

Rather than getting ready right away, Aubrey made her own breakfast and surfed the web. The building never seemed to run out of scalding hot water, so a flushing toilet or dishwasher running could turn a shower into a near-death experience.

Her wandering on the web led her to the same sites she'd used to find her internship. She considered contacting the company she had turned down to accept the position at Flare but decided to explore some more.

The apartment was situated such that the late fall sun shined in her bay windows for just a few minutes every morning. She had her back to it as she explored the jobs and internships available in New York. A beam of sunlight, which had been moving slowly across the floor and up her back, cleared her shoulder and hit the screen of her computer, turning it into a mirror. The look on her face startled her.

She was not looking at the excited girl who was sure she was headed for fame and fortune in the Big Apple. She wasn't even facing the anxious woman who was scrambling to find something, anything, to latch onto so she wouldn't have to admit defeat. The person she saw staring back at her was a sad, discouraged soul. An unemployed, uninterested New Yorker searching for a job and half-hoping not to find one. She closed the laptop.

As she showered and slowly dressed, she ran through her options. She really wasn't unemployed; she was unoccupied. Her financial situation was no different than it was when she walked out of Flare. If she wanted to make a little money, she could probably get a Christmas retail job. She could also apply for another internship. She could take a bold leap and take Tyrone up on his reference letter and try to get a paid position at a photography or design studio.

She thought about Joel and how he made her forget about her troubles. She thought about her parents' visits and how much easier it would be to appear employed as a photographer when she wasn't working at all. She was past fibbing now; she would do what she had to avoid letting Randall or Claire know what happened.

By the time she was dressed and back at her computer, she was a little happier and a lot more determined. She would enjoy Christmas, see where things went with Joel, spend quality time with her parents and start the New Year with a do-or-die-or-get-robbed-again attitude.

⤳

Joel: Hey. Busy later?

Aubrey: Meeting with Mayor B. Why?

Joel: Haha. You like trains?

Aubrey:	I guess
Joel:	Meet me at Anna's?
Aubrey:	When?
Joel:	1
Aubrey:	OK

Aubrey walked into the pizza parlor five minutes early and stood by the door. All of the tables were full and the sounds and smells of the lunch rush were pleasantly overwhelming. She watched Francis and his staff take orders, toss pizza crusts in the air, build pies, and work the oven. It was like a ballet. She took out her phone and began snapping pictures. Francis noticed her and lifted the hinged part of the counter and squeezed through.

She got ready to go into her stock "I'm a real photographer" speech in case he was one of the shy or cranky citizens she often ran into. He walked up to her and asked, "You Joel's friend? From the other day?"

"Yeah. He asked me to meet him here." She looked at her phone. "He's a couple minutes late."

"Come with me. You don't need to stand out here in the noise." He took her through the restaurant and into a small office in the very back. "Have a seat. Can I get you something?"

"Umm. No thanks. Joel should be here soon." Just as she said that, her phone vibrated.

Joel: Took a cab. Big mistake. Be there in 15.

"Well," she said, "Looks like he'll be a few more minutes." She stood up.

"Sit, sit. Let me make sure everything's running smooth out there and we can chat."

Aubrey was left wondering why the owner of a pizza joint was giving the VIP treatment to the new friend of a regular customer. *Joel must be quite the regular.*

"So," Francis said as he closed the door and sat in a cheap office chair on the other side of a small metal desk. "How long you known Joel?"

"A few days."

"Really? You looked like you been together a while."

"We're not really even together, I don't think."

He gave her a denture-perfect smile. "We'll see about that."

"How do you know him? If you don't mind me asking."

"Not at all. It's a great story. See, he came in here one day about six months . . . no, eight months ago—time flies!—and really liked the pizza. He started eating here a few times a week."

"Joel really likes pizza, huh?"

"I guess so! Anyway, he always came in when it was a little slow and we talked a few times. I told him how we were losing money and how close I was to having to close the place down." He paused and looked at a picture on his desk. "My Anna had the cancer. Between hospital bills and the money my no-good-cousin's son stole from me, I was tapped out."

Why are you telling me all this? Aubrey wondered.

"I still don't know why I told him the whole story. I guess he just has that kind of a face, you know? Like a guy you can trust. Anyway, he listens, but doesn't do the whole 'I'm sorry to hear that' schtick. He just listens."

"I think I know what you mean," Aubrey said, and it dawned on her that she already trusted Joel too. "He has an . . . an *air* about him."

"Yeah!" Francis lit up. "An *air*. So instead of giving me the sad sympathy face, he just takes his glasses off and says, 'You've got a great business here, Francis. I think we could make some money together.' This young kid with dried pizza sauce at the corner of his mouth wants to make money with me."

"Wow."

"Wow is right. A week later we were partners. He wrote me a really big check, biggest check I ever seen, and started giving me advice. Not like 'do what I say 'cause you're using my money,' but like a real partner. It's made all the difference."

"A big difference in a few months?"

"Yeah. He started using the Internet and the 'social media' stuff to promote the place. Now I've—we've—got more business than we can handle. Fingers crossed there's gonna be two more Anna's in the city by spring."

"So, the mystery man is some kind of tycoon, huh?"

"He had some sort of internet thing out in California. Cashed out big and moved here. I thank my lucky stars every day that he picked my place to have his first real slice."

A pimple-faced teenager stuck his head in the door. "Joel's here."

Aubrey and Francis stood up and Francis led her out of the office, yelling through the restaurant. "Back here, partner."

After dinner at Anna's New York Pizzeria, Joel ushered Aubrey into a cab. "2900 Southern Boulevard," Joel said to the driver, who looked back at him quizzically.

"Where's that?" Aubrey hadn't heard of Southern Boulevard.

"Ah. I was hoping you wouldn't recognize the address. That means there is at least one big New York experience you haven't had yet." He winked at the driver, who was watching them in the rearview mirror. "What was your favorite Christmas gift as a kid?"

"That's easy. My first camera."

"What kind? A film camera?"

"How old do you think I am? No, not a film camera. It was Nikon CoolPix. Not much compared to nowadays—my iPhone is a hundred times better—but it was a real camera."

"I remember those."

"Santa brought it to me when I was nine or ten. I started taking pictures of everything. By New Year's Day I'd filled up the hard drive on our computer." A touch of melancholy mixed with the excitement in her voice. "My dad said, 'You'll have to delete some. Keep your best ones and ditch the rest. There's only room for so many.' I asked why we couldn't just get a bigger computer. He told me that going through all my pictures would help me get good at taking pictures."

"Was he right?"

"Yeah. It took me a long time to realize it, but he was right. I still sometimes delete bad shots right after taking them even though I have room to store a million pictures. Okay, tell me about *your* favorite present."

"I was about the same age you were—nine, I think—when Santa brought me an electric train. Actually, Santa brought my dad an electric train and he let me play with it sometimes."

"Funny how that works, isn't it?"

"Turns out he always wanted one, but never got one for Christmas as a kid. It was apparently a big thing back in the day. By the time I got mine, it was a kind of unusual present."

"But you enjoyed it."

"Yeah, but not like you might think. Dad liked building a little world on a big piece of plywood and making it as realistic as possible. He had little buildings, cars, trees, even tiny people. I was fascinated by the *system*. About what the train was doing, how it knew where to go, how the trains kept from running into each other."

"You were a nerd."

"Absolutely and without apology. It gets better. The next year, we got our first computer. We always had one in the house, but it was for my parents' work and I wasn't allowed to touch it. On that next Christmas, we got one for the family."

"A train set and a computer. Did I mention that you were a nerd?"

He ignored the reminder. "Microsoft had a program—I think it's still available, actually—called Train Simulator."

"Oh. My. Goodness."

"That's right, I built super complicated train layouts on a computer while my dad played with the model train in the real world." He smiled at the memory. "Funny thing is, neither one of us rode a real train other than BART for a few more years."

"BART?"

"Bay Area Rapid Transit. It's the light rail system in the San Francisco area."

"So you've been on a real train since then?"

"Many. I still love 'em."

The cab pulled up in front of the New York Botanical Gardens. Aubrey blurted, "This place was next on my list!"

They walked through the big double doors of the conservatory and into the most amazing room Aubrey had ever seen. Dozens of trains ran along what looked like miles of track. Many of the New York City landmarks were included, but not as miniature versions of the original. Instead, they were artistic representations built from nature. The Brooklyn Bridge was made out of twigs, vines, and bark. Yankee Stadium was pinecones and pebbles. Everything was lit by a million tiny lights.

"Check this out," Joel said as he led her to a corner of the building.

"Cool!" Artists sat at workstations recreating the process they went through to build the huge display. "I wish I'd brought my real camera," she said.

Joel slid his backpack from his shoulder and said, "You didn't know we'd end up someplace this awesome. Luckily, I thought ahead." He gave her his Canon and watched her take picture after carefully composed picture.

After nearly two hours, the pair left the conservatory and explored some of the other exhibits. At some point, Aubrey took Joel's gloved hand in hers. On the ride back to Manhattan, she dozed off and her head tipped onto his shoulder.

Joel let it rest there.

She didn't mean to investigate him, she just thought their budding relationship was ready for Facebook. When no combination of "Joel, "Miller," "New York," or "California" led her to his page, she began to wonder. Did he not like Facebook? She tried Twitter. Nothing.

Her fingers perched over the keyboard, Aubrey asked herself if it was wrong to Google a potential boyfriend. Shouldn't she just ask him whatever questions she had? She could just text him and ask for his email address and if he had a Facebook page.

This is the internet age, she thought. *Everybody stalks everybody.* She typed his name in the search bar. The first three or four pages out of fifty million hits linked to lawyers, politicians, athletes, and, for some reason, a twelve-year-old little league player. She added "internet" and "millionaire," then "California" and even "trains." After an hour of scrolling through page after page of not-her-Joel, she closed the computer and went to bed.

Who are you, Joel Miller?

18 Days to Christmas

Joel and Aubrey ducked into a used bookstore as a cold, hard rain clattered through the downspouts. "Partly cloudy with a slight chance of rain, my eye," said a soaking-wet Aubrey.

"We should have known it was going to rain when the street vendors put away the fake designer sunglasses and set out the twenty dollar umbrellas."

"They are kind of psychic, aren't they?"

They sat for a few minutes in silence, watching New York City slow to what would still be a frantic pace in most other cities. Finally, Aubrey turned to Joel and asked, "What's your story, mystery man?"

"Mystery man? It's only a mystery because you haven't asked me before. You already know some of it, anyway."

"You told me you are from California and have been in New York for less than a year. Francis told me you 'cashed out' and invested in Anna's. That's pretty much it."

"A long time ago, in a galaxy far, far away . . ."

"Seriously."

"Okay. I grew up in northern California. My parents both teach school; Dad is a high school physics teacher and Mom is a professor at Stanford."

"That must make for interesting dinner conversation."

"You have no idea. I actually had my dad for a semester. That was fun. Then I went to Stanford."

"And had your mom as a professor," Aubrey interrupted.

"No, she teaches women's studies. That wasn't on my computer science course list."

"Computer science. Makes sense."

"It did at the time. I made it through two and a half years and then quit."

"Why?"

"It didn't make sense anymore. By the end of sophomore year I was running my own company. I learned more on my own in a month than Stanford was teaching me in a year."

"Was that the company you cashed out or whatever before you came here?"

"Yes and no. The company and I actually parted ways quite a while before I sold my patents."

"Patents?"

"I had a cool idea while I was working on one of my school projects. It turns out nobody had seen things quite the way I did. A little bit like you and your photos, I guess. Anyway, a very wise advisor helped me protect the idea."

"What was it?"

"It's hard to explain because it's not a thing by itself. It's a way for phones and computers to communicate." He held out his hand. "Let me see your phone."

She handed it to him. He slid in close beside her and held it so she could see the screen while he worked it.

"Wow. You have a lot of apps here."

"I'm kind of an app hoarder."

"My process—it's not mine anymore, I guess—but the process I came up with isn't an app. It makes other apps work better and faster." He pointed to an icon on the screen. "This one uses it . . . and this one . . . and this one . . ." He navigated to the next screen. ". . . And this one . . . and this one . . ." Another screen ". . . and this one . . . and this one."

"Are you serious?"

"Yeah. I think that's it. No wait, this one uses it too, I think."

"So every time someone buys one of those apps you get a quarter or something?"

"More like a penny. Used to be, anyway. I sold the patents to a holding company. All they do is own and license patents."

"If so many apps use your idea, it must've been worth a lot."

"Let's just say the check had a few zeros on it."

"So, let's see if I have this right. You were a big Silicon Valley millionaire and gave it all up to move to New York and make pizza."

"That's one way to look at it, I guess. I just didn't want to be out there anymore. Silicon Valley is like high school in bizarro world."

Aubrey furrowed her brow.

Joel explained, "You know, bizarro world. Where everything is backwards. The nerds are kings and the jocks—people with 'normal' jobs like doctors and lawyers—are the outcasts. Trust me, give a geek some money and power and he can be just as petty and ruthless as anybody. I got tired of hearing about the next startup. The next round of venture funding. The companies formed and incubated just so they could sell to Google or Apple or Yahoo and make some twenty-year-old a millionaire."

"Isn't that what you did?"

"Exactly. I was in the right place at the right time with a pretty good idea. There's no way it was worth all the money the brokers got for me. I came out here to see what I could do in the real world."

"Pizza."

"Pizza."

"That's a great story." Aubrey didn't know she was still scowling.

"What's wrong?"

"It's almost too great a story."

"Like hard-to-believe too great a story?"

"Kind of." She thought about her time with Google. *There's no way his name wouldn't come up if he did everything he just said he did.*

Joel mirrored her sour look. "I guess it is kind of far-fetched."

"Plus . . ." Aubrey hesitated.

"Plus what?"

"You might think this is weird or whatever, but I looked for you on the Internet."

"That's not weird. What did you find? Is there a Joel Miller out there who tortures puppies or something?"

"I didn't find you at all. Nothing."

He smiled. "And yet you met me again. That's awesome."

"You aren't bothered that I stalked you? That your story somehow escaped the internet?"

He took out his wallet and handed Aubrey a business card.

JOLE MULLER. Serial Entrepreneur.

"Jole Muller? Not J-o-e-l M-i-l-l-e-r?"

"I never said 'Miller.' That's just what you heard."

"Well, I've never heard of the name Jole."

"It is unique. I've only met one other and her parents picked letters out of a hat. Seriously."

"Jole Muller. That explains why I didn't find you on Facebook or Google. Where did 'Jole' come from?"

"My parents were wannabe hippies. They were just born a little too late. But they were really into stuff that happened in the sixties. And I was born on October ninth."

"What's special about October ninth?"

He rolled his eyes. "Never ask that question in front of my parents or any other rabid Beatles fan."

"Still nothing."

"It's John Lennon's birthday. My mom wanted to name me John Lennon Muller, but my dad thought it was a little much. So they got California creative."

"Jole!" Aubrey exclaimed. "J-o from John and l-e from Lennon."

"Give the gorgeous girl a prize."

11 Days to Christmas

She didn't know it at the time, but the next week was one of the best weeks of the whole year. She not only Googled Jole Muller—with him by her side to filter out the untruths—but she got to really know him. His comment about being in the right place at the right time made sense to her as she tried to imagine him as an arrogant cyber aristocrat. He really was, she decided, simply a nice guy who had a great idea that made him a lot of money.

They spent most of every day together from the time they walked out of a bookstore onto a street glistening with rain water until the day her mother arrived at JFK airport.

"Do you want me to come with you to pick her up?"

"Oh, no. If she sees us together, she will have us married by the end of the cab ride home." She watched him to see how he would react to the word *married*. He didn't. *You should take some of your money to Vegas and play poker.*

"That makes sense. My grandmother wouldn't have us married, but she would definitely grill me."

"Actually, I don't know how I'm going to make these next couple of days work. Mom doesn't know I got fired."

"Why not?"

"It's complicated. In fact, she thinks I work for real money. My dad too."

Jole pursed his lips together and adjusted his glasses. "I'm sure you'll make it work. You want me to lie low while she's here?"

"Yes. No. She and I are going to spend a lot of time together, but I also have to go to 'work' some."

"Complicated."

Aubrey was becoming increasingly uncomfortable. "Sorry, Jole. I told you a lot about my folks, but we're still dealing with a lot of baggage. You'll just have to roll with it for a while. I think I'm doing the right thing."

"Who am I to say otherwise? My parents don't even know where I am."

❧

Claire was standing patiently by the baggage claim when Aubrey finally found her. The flight information changed between the last time Aubrey checked and when the bags were actually dumped at the carrousel. "Sorry I'm late," she said as she hugged her mother. Claire was wearing a new perfume.

"I was beginning to think you forgot about me," Claire answered with a smile. "Is the cab still waiting?"

"There is no cab. I took the subway and train. I thought it would be a fun way for us to get around."

"Oh, no, dear. I can't possibly drag this bag around on public transportation." She pointed to a large wheeled suitcase.

Are you moving in? Aubrey thought. "Makes sense. Let's head out to the cab line, then."

They chatted for the few minutes they had to wait. The sun was bright and warm on Aubrey's face, but the wind, funneled along the front of the building, cut through her jacket. She was glad to climb into the cab next to her mother.

Claire was quiet. As the cab turned and the Manhattan skyline filled the window on her mother's side of the car, Aubrey said, "It's so packed. The city, I mean. It's like they took ten copies of downtown Dallas and squished them together to fit on the island."

"I don't want to talk about Dallas."

Aubrey knew Claire really meant she *needed* to talk about Dallas. "Why not? What's going on?"

Without turning away from the window, Claire answered, "Randall cheated on me."

"No . . . really? Why do you think that?"

"Some friends from work and I went downtown for lunch last week. I'm hardly ever in that part of town—he probably counted on that—and there he was. There *they were* all cozy. He was closer to that woman than he'd been to me for years and years."

"Mom, you're not married anymore. Dad going to lunch with another woman isn't exactly cheating."

"I know that! I know that. But it was Diane from his firm. You remember her, don't you? Slinky little redhead lawyer shooting for . . ." she spit out the word ". . . *partner.*"

"No, I don't remember her. I'm still not sure how going to lunch with a coworker is cheating on an ex-wife."

111

"They were real friendly before the divorce. I asked him about her. He denied any monkey business, of course, but I always wondered about that Diane." She took a long breath and appeared to gather in a memory. "It was the one thing we promised we'd never do. Even when we dated we talked about it. 'No matter what,' he'd said, 'true fidelity to the end. As long as I have your ring on my finger, I will be true.' I can hear him saying it all these years and lies later."

"So you think he was having an *affair* while you were still married?"

Claire nodded her head.

Aubrey continued, "Did you ask him about it last week?"

"I was too embarrassed to confront him in front of my friends. I tried to call him, but he didn't answer."

"Mom, I can see why you'd be upset running into Dad and Diane. But you have to admit that you do have a tendency to put two and two together and get five. Remember when you thought my first real boyfriend was a drug dealer?"

"You'll never let me live that one down, will you? This thing with Randall is different. Now that I think of it, I missed other clues." She didn't wait for a "like what?" and went on. "For instance, when he had to work late or travel, he would usually tell me who he was going to be with. But sometimes, he didn't. Sometimes I would ask and he'd roll his eyes or ignore me. It seemed to start right when that woman started working at the firm."

"You have got to talk to him, Mom. He's done a lot to let me and you down, but don't you think he still deserves a chance to explain?"

"I doubt he'll want to talk about it. He probably knows he's in trouble."

"Trouble?"

"My lawyer says I can revisit the settlement if I can prove he lied at the deposition. Plus, that's perjury. He could be disbarred."

"You'd do that to him?"

"I don't know. Maybe." She turned toward Aubrey. The running mascara and quivering red lips said she was more hurt than angry.

"Oh, Mom, I'm so sorry." Aubrey slipped an arm around her mother's shoulder, their coats creating an awkward buffer between them.

"It's okay. I wasn't even going to tell you. I came here to be with my Aubrey and have some New York fun."

"That we can do."

Aubrey pushed open the door to her freshly cleaned apartment. "Ta-dah!"

"Oh, isn't it precious." Claire wheeled her bag to the tiny bed and hefted it up onto the comforter. "You're sure you want me to sleep on the bed? I can take the . . ."

"The *what*, Mom?" Aubrey laughed and spread her arms. "I'll be fine on the floor for a couple of nights. I still have the air mattress I used when I first got here."

"We were happy then, weren't we?"

"Huh?"

Claire pointed to a photograph on the wall next to the bed. Aubrey had put it out just a few days earlier. It was a close-up shot of a pair of gloved hands making a snowball. They were Randall's hands, and the snowball was about to be playfully tossed at Claire. She had slipped as she tried to duck and ended up sprawled in the fluffy snow. Aubrey joined her and they made snow angels.

Aubrey smiled at the memory. "Yeah, I guess we were."

Claire reached out to touch the edge of the picture frame. "At least I was happy most of the time. I guess you were too. I hope you were happy. If you ask Randall, he was already pretending by then."

"When did you start pretending, Mom?"

Claire shook her head. "Sorry. I didn't mean to bring it up. Let's get going. We're going to shop the whole length of Fifth Avenue."

Aubrey nodded and wondered how many of those conversations she could survive before the cab ride home.

Arm in arm, they walked the few blocks to Macy's. Claire's head was on a tourist's swivel as she took in the massive movement and imposing noise of the churning crowds and traffic. Aubrey was looking around too, but more subtly and cautiously. Any New Yorker would have recognized the pair as tourist and protective guide.

Aubrey began to get excited as they approached the store. She had walked by a couple of days before and taken a quick look at some of the window displays. She couldn't wait to see how her mother reacted. "Look, Mom, your first New York Christmas window displays." She swung her Nikon around on its strap and began taking pictures.

"Oh, my, they take their window dressing serious here, don't they?" Claire approached a window separating her from a Victorian era drawing room. A well-dressed family surrounded a ten-foot-tall tree. It was decorated with antique ornaments and very realistic flickering candles. "I wonder what they want for that bag," Claire said as she pushed through the door next to the window.

Aubrey spent the next four hours following her mother between and through the stores. They walked along Fifth Avenue through midtown Manhattan all the way to Central Park. "It's going to be dark soon, Mom. Would you like to sit in the park for a bit?"

"No, dear. Let's visit a couple more stores and then get something to eat." They ended up in Bloomingdale's, and they went through the exact routine established many stores earlier.

Claire would pick up something she thought Aubrey should have.

Aubrey would say she didn't have anywhere to wear/carry/use it.

Claire would insist and Aubrey would sigh and thank her mother.

By the time they settled into Dawat for Indian food, Aubrey felt like a pack mule. They sat at a table for four with bags sitting on and under the other two chairs. The camera sat on the table across from Aubrey where she could keep an eye on it. "My dogs are barking," Aubrey said, quoting Francis while wishing she were eating pizza instead of chicken makhani.

"Hmm? Where did *that* come from?"

"A new friend. It means my feet hurt."

"I figured what it meant, dear, I just haven't ever heard it before. It's cute."

"Uh-huh. How's your dinner?"

"Delightful. I could get used to the shopping and eating here. I'm a bit jealous of you."

"It's not too bad, I guess. I do miss the quiet sometimes."

"The grass is always greener . . ."

Claire paid the check and asked the waitress how to order a cab. Aubrey jumped in. "Mom, we just go outside and wave one down. It might take a couple of minutes because it's busy, but you never have to 'order' one around here."

A cab was dropping an elderly couple off just as Claire and Aubrey wrestled their packages through the restaurant door. Aubrey held up a handful of bags and gave the driver a vigorous nod. He stayed in the driver's seat for a few seconds until he must have noticed Claire's designer clothes. Then he jumped out, opened the trunk, and helped the pair with their shopping bags.

Aubrey gave him the address and he pulled off with a jolt. Just after he turned back onto Fifth Avenue, Claire let out a squeal. "Stop! Right here. Let us out."

A very annoyed cab driver pulled over and looked at Aubrey in the mirror as if to say, "Are you really with this crazy lady?" Aubrey pulled out a twenty and handed it over to him as he got out to unload the trunk again.

"What are we doing, Mom?" Claire was looking across the street with a sly grin on her face.

"Come with me." Aubrey realized where they were headed before they'd gotten all the way across the busy street. Right on the corner next to Trump Tower sat a building that looked much like a bank. It was starting to get dark, but she could still make out the words carved in the stone above the front doors: "Tiffany and Co."

"Where are we going, Mom? Don't you think we've shopped enough?" Just as she asked the question, the doorway and windows burst into light as thousands of tiny bulbs came alive.

"Ooooh," Claire answered.

"Mother, we just walked past this place a couple hours ago."

"But I just had a wonderful idea. Did you bring that card Randall gave you?"

Aubrey instantly regretted putting it in her wallet a few days before. "I think so."

"Wonderful." The tone of her voice made Aubrey think of the Grinch. She watched who she thought was her mother tilt her nose into the air and wait for a young man in a suit to open and hold the enormous door for them. He and a young woman took their bags and disappeared.

A woman about Claire's age came out from behind the counter. Aubrey could feel herself being sized up. "How can I help you today?"

Claire looked at her daughter. "Her father is going to buy her a very nice Christmas present this evening."

The woman seemed to either understand what was going on or not care. "Very nice. Are we looking for earrings, or, might I suggest, a spectacular necklace."

"A necklace, don't you think, dear?"

Aubrey whispered, "Mom, what are you doing?"

She whispered back, "He owes you."

"No, he doesn't. You think he owes *you*."

"Either way. He's buying you a very expensive necklace."

"No, he's not. I'm leaving. Are you coming with me?"

Claire stood trapped between her determined daughter and half the staff of Tiffany's. Her face softened, but she did not move.

Aubrey turned toward the door. "I'll be outside."

Ten minutes later, four people came out of Tiffany's. Three of them were smiling. Claire was not. "Here. Merry Christmas." She handed Aubrey a blue box as the perfect pair of young workers set the shopping bags on the sidewalk.

The saleswoman chimed in like a commercial. "Yes. Merry Christmas. You're going to absolutely love it."

Aubrey dropped the box into one of the bags and hailed a cab. The only words spoken between the jewelry store and Aubrey's apartment came from Claire's downturned lips. "Don't worry about Randall's bank account. *I* bought you the necklace."

The tiny apartment amplified the awkwardness of the evening. Claire read a book. Aubrey carried a basket of clean clothes she just hadn't put away yet back to the basement. "I've got some laundry to do. I'll be back in a while. You think about what you want to do tomorrow."

Aubrey had already decided what *she* was going to do in the morning. She plopped on the dirty floor and called Jole from laundry room. "Hey. What's up?"

"How is it going with your mom?"

"Okay. Maybe we can talk about it tomorrow over breakfast?"

"What about . . ."

"She'll be fine."

"Sure. Text me after eight."

Claire was in the bathroom getting ready for bed when Aubrey got back to the apartment. She came out with her face scrubbed and her hair tied back in a scrunchy. *When did my mother get so old?*

"I suspect I overdid things this afternoon," Claire said as she got into the bed. "I should have paced myself a little better."

"You're probably dragging from the flight too."

"Yes, I'm sure that's part of it."

"We'll take it a little easier tomorrow."

"Mmm-hmm."

"You sleep in as long as you like. I'll go out and get us breakfast in the morning."

"Thank you, dear. Goodnight."

10 Days to Christmas

The bagels were still warm when Aubrey pulled them out of the white paper bag and put them on a plate. At some point during the fifteen-minute trip, Claire went from a deep snoring sleep to up and in the shower. Aubrey needed a little more time before starting day two. "Mom?" she said through the door.

"Yes?"

"I gotta go to work real quick and take care of something. I'll be back in an hour or so. Think about what you want to do today."

Silence.

"Okay?" Only the sound of running water came from the bathroom. "Mom?"

"That's fine, dear. I'll see you later."

"Breakfast is on the table."

She went right back to the deli where she'd bought the breakfast bagels. Jole was waiting. "Hungry?"

"Not really." Looking at the scrambled egg sandwich Jole bought changed her stomach's mind. "On second thought . . . is that for me?"

"Sure is. Help yourself. I got that and a plain one. You get first choice." He buttered his toasted bagel and spread several tablespoons of cream cheese on it.

"Butter *and* cream cheese?"

"You only live once," he said as he took a big bite. He chewed and waited until Aubrey had finished her first bite. "How's it going with your mom? She thinks you're at work, right?"

"Yeah. We had an argument yesterday. It's not the best visit in the world, at least so far."

Jole took another bite and chewed slowly.

Aubrey continued, "She thinks my dad had an affair while they were still married." She tried to swallow the words back in. *Why am I telling him this?*

"She must be pretty upset."

"Seems to be. I think she's overreacting a bit, though."

"Really?"

"That's probably not the right way to say it. Jumping to conclusions is more like it."

"Still."

"Still, I guess I would be upset too."

"You're not?"

"A little. But right now I'm as annoyed at her as I am at him. She swept into town and took me along on her shopping therapy. It's not what I pictured."

"Hmm. It's none of my business."

It's none of your business . . . but . . .

There was no "but." He simply finished his bagel and said, "I've got business over in Jersey. You're welcome to tag along if you need to be at 'work' for a few hours."

"No. I shouldn't leave her alone that long." Aubrey imagined her mother standing in front of the snowball picture.

"All right. See you later then."

Aubrey sat at the narrow counter for a few more minutes before taking the subway uptown. She tried to put herself in her mother's position. Since the divorce, Aubrey had wondered how much of it was Aubrey's fault. Claire must be wondering how much was Claire's fault even as she worked so hard to make it all Randall's fault. Now it might be Diane's fault.

Or not.

Aubrey came out of the subway at Columbus Circle and dialed her mother's cell phone number.

"Hello?"

"Hey, Mom, it's me. I'm wrapping up here and about to head home."

"Oh."

"Sorry about last night, but I just hate getting between you and Dad."

"That's one thing you have in common."

"What?"

"The 'but apology.'"

"I don't get it."

"You know. Randall never apologized without putting a 'but' in there somewhere. 'Sorry I'm late, but something came up at work. Sorry I snapped at you, but you hit my last nerve. Sorry I moved out, but we just can't do this anymore.'"

"Mom, you have every right to be upset with Dad . . . and me. Let's talk about it when I get there."

"No, let's not. Not yet. I'm really, really sorry, Aubrey. I ruined your day yesterday. I behaved terribly. I should have just stayed in Dallas until this latest thing with your father—whatever it turns out to be—was worked out."

"I didn't handle it well either, Mom."

Silence.

"I'll be there soon and we can figure out what to do next. Okay?"

"See you later, Aubrey."

The call ended as Aubrey headed back down into the subway. She got off early and jogged a few blocks instead of changing trains. A cab pulled away as she ran up to her building.

As she feared, the apartment was empty. The bed was made and a note on the pillow read, "Sweetheart, sorry I missed you. I got an early flight out. I'm sorry I rained on your Christmas parade. Call me Sunday. Everything is going to be okay. With love, Mom."

Five shopping bags stood neatly at the foot of the bed. The store receipts were lying flat on top of the purchases in each bag. Aubrey was tempted to gather everything up and go reverse shopping. She didn't *need* anything Claire insisted on buying. If it weren't for the receipts, in fact, Aubrey would only remember the contents of a few of the Christmas-wrapped presents. She didn't even know for sure what was in the blue box from Tiffany's. *That one is definitely going back.*

She decided to keep the rest; she couldn't bear the thought of her mother getting her credit card statement and seeing all the returns. She stacked the gifts next to the window in the shape of a Christmas tree.

The largest packages on the bottom supported a triangle of smaller ones. The velvet bow from the Tiffany's box served as a star on top of the stack. She took a few pictures and then removed the memory card from her camera.

After transferring all the images to the computer, she began the painstaking process of cataloging them. As always, her pictures made her relive the moments around them. When she got to the series of window displays she took while her mother was inside the stores, shopping, she recalled how alone she felt. She doubted Claire even realized several minutes went by before Aubrey joined her in each store.

Macy's, Lord and Taylor, Saks, Bergdorf Goodman, Barney's, Bloomingdale's. Each window display was vibrant and whimsical. Aubrey's pictures were perfectly focused and beautifully composed. She should have been proud of her work, but she wasn't. She launched a photo sharing site in her web browser and typed "Macy's Christmas window display" in the search bar. Just like Jole's first picture of Rockefeller Center, a dozen images similar to Aubrey's popped onto the screen.

Something caught her eye in the corner of one of her pictures. She zoomed in and spotted a hole the size of a dime in the ankle of one of the mannequins at Macy's. She reframed and cropped the picture so a viewer's eye would be drawn to the hole, which now filled nearly a quarter of the frame. It wasn't a perfect Christmas window display any more. Now it was a well-used mannequin pressed into service for yet another December.

Aubrey went back through all the pictures she took during the shopping trip. Some she turned into black and white. Others she cropped or flipped, or changed the color palette. When she was finished, she had a collection of photographs that were obviously taken at Christmastime, but weren't Christmas pictures.

Somehow, she felt oddly proud of her very un-Christmas collection.

7 Days to Christmas

*A*fter her experience with Claire, Aubrey was certainly not looking forward to Randall's visit. When she got his text telling her he was at his hotel, she almost didn't answer it. Just as she gave in and was about to respond, another message came in.

Dad: Just had great idea. Cool display at Met. Still have
        time tonight. Game?

Aubrey dialed his number. "Hey, Dad, welcome to New York."

"Glad to be here. Should be a great visit. We're going to close this deal and take the client to the next level."

"I'm sure you will. Tell me about the museum thing. I haven't heard about it."

"Guy on the plane told me. Every year the Met has a tree and a few Christmas things, but this year they set up a whole section of the museum. 'Christmas Americana,' or something like that."

"Are you sure you want to do a museum? It's awfully close to artsy. Plus, the Metropolitan Museum of Art and the Metropolitan Opera are both called 'The Met.' We might accidentally end up in the wrong one."

"I don't think so. My cowboy ESP won't let me get within a mile of an opera—or ballet, for that matter—without giving me the willies."

Aubrey laughed despite herself. "Okay, but we better get over there. The museums are one of the few things that close at a reasonable hour in this city."

"Right. I'm close enough to hoof it. See you in fifteen? Can you get there that fast?"

"Not quite. More like half an hour."

"I look forward to seeing you, Aubrey."

"Me too."

She hung up, put on a nicer top and her coat, and grabbed her camera. As she walked to the subway, she tried to decide how to deal with the Diane Question. Did Claire finally confront him after she got back to Dallas? Does Randall know that Aubrey knows? Does it matter? She finally decided to pretend she didn't know anything unless he brought it up. With any luck, he wouldn't.

This was either going to be one of the best times she ever had with her father or one of the absolute worst. She wanted to expect the best, but as the tunnels and platforms moved past the window, she had a sinking feeling.

She was not feeling lucky.

⌒⊙

She shouldn't have been surprised to get to the museum before her father. Even though she rode all the way uptown from Chelsea and her father was walking from a nearby hotel—the Clairmont, Plaza, or Four Seasons, most likely—he managed to be late.

Aubrey admired and photographed the tree in the foyer while keeping one eye on the entrance. She composed her shots with an eye toward building a collection like the one she made of the window displays. She searched for flaws and anomalies. Streaks and stains. Chips and cracks.

Randall still managed to sneak up on her. "Howdy, youngin'."

His big smile caught her off guard. "Daddy!" She mashed her camera into his chest as she gave him a hug.

"Ouch. Careful of the old breadbasket. That can't be good for your camera either."

"Sorry. You surprised me."

"That's hard to believe. Now, if I'd been here fifteen minutes ago, you might have been surprised."

"True."

"I hope you didn't buy tickets. I stopped by earlier and picked up a pair."

"Nope. I figured you would have it all set up."

They handed their tickets to a matronly woman, who pointed at her watch. "We close in an hour, but we clear the galleries in forty-five minutes."

"Yes, ma'am," Randall answered as he tipped his imaginary cowboy hat. He asked Aubrey, "You think we can see a couple hundred Christmases in forty-five minutes?"

"I guess we'll see."

They started in seventeenth century Jamestown and worked their way up to examples of how soldiers celebrated Christmas during the Civil War. The decorations were beautiful in their simplicity. Aubrey was excited to capture items that were perfect and yet flawed. The tool and brush marks on a carefully painted carving of Santa Claus from the late 1800s were clear in Aubrey's viewfinder. The muted red and black of his clothing would be unacceptable in the window of Bloomingdale's, but were the very best a loving craftsman had to offer in his day.

Randall was doing only slightly better than his ex-wife at exploring with Aubrey. He was usually an exhibit or two ahead of her. He finally stopped at the entrance to the final room and waited for his daughter and her camera. "You know they sell books with pictures of all these things."

"I don't have a coffee table." She looked carefully to see if he was joking or prodding.

"Ah, I see. Well, maybe you should make a coffee table book out of your pictures. Then you could sell a few copies and buy yourself a coffee table."

"Great idea. I might even have a few dollars left over to buy a couple of coffee table books."

"Come on. We have twenty minutes and over a hundred years to cover."

They worked their way through the century, looking at the decorations, paintings, cards, and gifts that made Christmas special during the brightest and darkest winters of America's twentieth century. As they got closer to recent times, Aubrey began to connect with things she recognized. When they got to the nineties, memories of real Porter family Christmases took over the front of her mind.

Claire fussing at Randall for giving Aubrey a Polly Pocket. "She's too little. She can choke on the tiny pieces."

"Nonsense. She is smart enough to tell the difference between a carrot and a plastic girl."

A "collector's edition" Beanie Baby Randall had used to explain investing. "Take good care of that raccoon, Aubrey. If you do, it will be worth some money when you get older."

She was now taking pictures of her childhood. A tear got trapped between her eye and her camera when she saw Samantha. By the time Santa left her under the tree, Aubrey was too old for dolls or Santa. A whole closetful of Barbies sat alone and neglected. Samantha was different. She became Aubrey's confidant. The American Girl doll sat proudly at the head of the bed, unless friends were over. Then, Aubrey would apologize to her before putting her gently in a drawer.

Randall noticed his daughter stopped at the exhibit. "Bet you wish you still had her, don't you?"

Aubrey blinked the tear away and answered, "Hmm?"

"That doll. I bought it from a friend because the stores were sold out. Turns out it was one of the first ones made. It's probably worth a few hundred bucks."

"Seriously, Dad?"

"What?"

"Think about it. We're standing here in the middle of a dozen Porter Christmases and you think about what my doll might be worth? In money?"

"Sorry. I didn't know what you were thinking about."

"That's okay. I shouldn't expect you to read my mind. It's just a little hard."

"The divorce."

"Not just that. It's hard getting used to my new parents." She waved over the toys. "The parents around during these Christmases are gone. I don't have a mom and dad any more, really. I love you guys, but I have to figure out what we are now."

"We're still a family, Aubrey. Just a different flavor."

"That's not how it works, Dad. We're not talking about strawberry versus cherry. I don't know you. I look at you and Mom and replay the years, searching for clues that should have told me what was happening to us."

Randall's mouth opened and shut, but no words came out. Aubrey let him squirm for a few awkward seconds and then walked past him and toward the museum exit. A picture of the back of her mother's head taken through the rear window of a taxi popped into her mind. She stopped, turned, smiled gently—*sorry, Daddy*—and waited for Randall to catch up.

After a pleasant dinner free of any discussion beyond what two coworkers might chat about, Aubrey and Randall said goodnight. "My big meeting is at ten in the morning, and we'll need time to get prepped for it. If you're still interested, I can call you after lunch and we can do something."

"Ice skating?" Aubrey asked tentatively.

"Sure. Why not."

As her father walked away, Aubrey wondered who made up the "we" he said had to get ready for the meeting. Was it Diane? She wanted to know, but didn't want to ask.

6 Days to Christmas

The sun and morning sounds woke Aubrey up at around nine. She had gotten into the habit of staying up late and not setting an alarm. It was after two a.m. when she finished editing the pictures from the museum and finally went to bed. She was trying to convince herself she was a night owl, but it wasn't working for her. She was exhausted when she went to bed and tired when she got up. She'd been trying afternoon naps, but they made her feel unemployed.

She wasn't sure she was looking forward to spending the afternoon with her father. The peaceful dinner conversation, she feared, was a fluke. Would they— she—be able to keep the monsters in a box for a few more hours?

Her phone buzzed.

Jole: In your part of town. Coffee in the park?
Aubrey: Which park?
Jole: Chelsea.

Jole really *was* in her part of town, practically outside her door. She told him to meet her in fifteen minutes and then rushed through her morning routine.

He was waiting for her, wrapped in his trademark rich nerd winter wear. This time the jeans were Wrangler and the coat an expensive puffy black North Face parka.

"Going mountain climbing later?"

"Yes, as a matter of fact." He handed her a large Starbucks cup. "Here. After we finish these, I'll have the Sherpas fetch a couple more." He was smiling, but his words had a slight wintery sharpness to them.

"Thanks, Jole." She took the cup with both hands and used it to warm them. "I should have worn gloves. It's colder than it looks from inside."

"True, true. Even my thousand-dollar mountaineering mittens barely keep my hands warm." Another blast of arctic wind.

Aubrey wanted to change the subject, but had no idea where to go. She took another sip of the coffee. "Thanks again. This is great. Thanks for calling me."

"You're welcome. I missed seeing you the past couple days. How did it go with your dad?"

"It's still going. We went to the museum and dinner last night. It was okay. Today we're supposed to go ice skating."

"That sounds like fun."

"Could be. We'll see. He has a big meeting this morning, and who knows what will come up between now and after lunch."

"How's your mom doing?"

"I don't know. We haven't spoken since she left. We're supposed to chat on Sunday." She leaned away from Jole almost imperceptibly. "Why do you ask?"

"Sorry. It's none of my business."

"That's twice you've said that. I know we're at an awkward point in whatever this is between us, but shouldn't we figure out what is whose business?"

"I'm not used to any of this, Aubrey. Most of the relationships I've been in over the past few years have been short-lived and shallow. And I'm not just talking boy-girl relationships. Money changes the game, you know?"

"Believe it or not, I do kind of know. We're not Internet *super*-rich, but most people would call my family upper class. People treat you differently."

"Yeah. So I don't have a lot of practice living in that space between new friend and close confidant. Plus, I don't want to complicate things between us too much."

"Trust me, Jole, this may feel complicated to you, but right now, this is the *least* complicated relationship I'm living in." She put her hand on his arm. "Talk to me."

"You're sure?"

Aubrey wasn't. She looked at her reflection in Jole's glasses. Her face floated, translucent, in front of his gorgeous blue eyes. His warmth escaped his puffy coat into her hand. She wanted him to tell her everything she was doing was right. She wanted him to tell her he had strong feelings for her and they would be something together. Still, she feared he wasn't going to say any of those things. She finally answered, "Yes. I'm sure."

"It sounds to me like you're being a little hard on your parents. It's Christmastime for them too. They don't have each other *or* you this year." He paused and waited for Aubrey to answer. She pulled her hand into her lap and stared at it. Jole continued, "My parents were good protectors and providers. Their marriage does what they want it to do. But you've described more of what I imagine a family to be. Something I haven't had my whole life. That's part of why my new home is twenty-five hundred miles away from my old home."

Aubrey looked at him again. "You ran away from home."

He smiled. "Yeah. I guess I did. I want Jole Muller to be part of a traditional American family even if I'm the only one in it. So it makes me . . . I don't know . . . it's uncomfortable to watch you work against your parents."

Work against my parents? Aubrey thought. "I get your point, but you only see a small corner of the picture. They pretended to be a traditional American family. I left for college thinking I was the kid of a happy couple. Then I found out I was the reason an unhappy couple lied to their kid."

"Okay. You're right. See? I don't know enough to meddle. How about we take our families off the list of things we talk about? At least for a while."

"Sure. Thanks for the coffee. And the conversation." She stood. "I gotta go ice skating."

❧

"How did your meeting go?"

"We killed it," Randall said. "I just hope we didn't bite off more than we can chew."

"Is that even possible for you?"

"I'll take that obnoxious question as a compliment. It is a big deal, though. Good for the firm."

"You still good to go skating?"

"Absolutely. Wouldn't miss it for anything."

"Cool. Meet me at Rockefeller Center?"

Pause. "Sure. When?"

"Half an hour." She sucked in a breath and added, "Just the two of us?"

"Unless you're bringing someone."

"No. You just said you had someone with you. I thought you might be doing the tourist thing with them."

"Oh. No. We're pretty much on our own outside of the meeting we just had."

"Great. See you in a while."

I still don't know if Diane is here, Aubrey thought. She bundled up and headed for the subway. *And I still don't know if I even care.*

A man and his young daughter got to the stairs just before she did. They walked down slowly, side by side, hand in hand. Aubrey and several others were caught behind them. A woman behind Aubrey muttered, "Seriously?" Aubrey paused long enough to let the pair ahead of her put a couple more stairs between them. She shifted from side to side so the mutterer couldn't pass her on the stairway. *That will teach you to complain, my friend.*

Aubrey and the father-daughter pair got on the same train. She watched as he took her little mittens and put them in his pocket. The girl grinned and swung her feet back and forth. In another few months, Aubrey thought, those feet would be touching the floor.

Are you as happy as you look? How's the marriage? Is your daughter going to wake up one day and learn today was counterfeit?

She shook her head and took out her phone. She held it up and stared at it as if doing something very important. She took a picture of a smiling father with his arm around his enchanted daughter. Later, she would enlarge the image and try to see behind the faces.

Randall was waiting for her at the top of the stairs when she came up out of the subway. He was actually wearing a cowboy hat. "Did you wear that to your big meeting?"

"No. In fact, I'll need you to keep a secret for me."

"Okay . . ."

He leaned down and whispered, "I bought this here. Just around the corner. Who'd'a thought I'd find such a great hat outside of Texas?"

They joined the throng of tourists and frustrated locals all walking toward the center of Rockefeller Plaza. Before they could even see the rink, the crowd stopped. Some people squeezed past, but others seemed content to just stand there. Aubrey saw the black posts and long straps set up to corral the potential skaters. "I guess this is the line."

"Can't be. We're a mile back."

"It's not that far, Dad. I don't think there is much room inside so people have to line up out here. Plus, in a few minutes, we can watch while we wait."

"Are you sure you wouldn't rather go to one of the rinks in Central Park? The lines can't be as long as this."

"Come on, Dad. We're finally at Rock Center a week before Christmas. How many times does a chance like this come around?"

Randall shrugged. "Whatever you want, Aubrey." He put a long arm around her shoulders and squeezed. "Whatever you want."

After just a few minutes, they made it to the railing where they could look down on the rink. It seemed a thousand people were waiting their turn to be one of fifty on the ice. Randall was fidgeting. Aubrey tried to distract him. "I wish I'd brought my real camera."

"You can still go and get it. I'll hold our place in line. Just be sure to hurry back. Looks like we'll be down there in four or five hours."

"Ha. Ha. So tell me about work. What's going on besides the big deal you just closed?"

"The usual boring lawyer stuff. I'm working like an intern right now, sixty, seventy hours some weeks. A side effect of not having anyplace to go at the end of the day."

Randall continued, "What about you? How's your job going? How did you get yesterday *and* today off?"

Uh-oh. Why did I mention work?

"Just lucky. I actually had to go in while Mom was here. My hours are a lot more flexible lately. I expect to have a more normal routine after New Year's."

"What do you do, exactly?"

"At first, there was a lot of on-the-job training. Busywork, you know? My last assignment was actually right here. They asked me to take pictures of the tree lighting."

"Impressive. So . . . do you have any New York friends yet? Anyone from work?"

"A couple of new acquaintances. Maybe a potential friend or two. How about you? Any new friends in your life?" *Maybe someone named Diane?*

"Not really."

Let it go, Aubrey. "Oh. I just thought a newly single man might be making new friends."

"Objection, Your Honor. Fishing expedition."

"Never mind."

"I recognize that tone, Aubrey Porter. Something's on your mind." He looked around at the strangers surrounding them.

"Do you have a girlfriend?" Aubrey asked quietly, almost under her breath.

"Normally I would say that's none of your business, but since you asked so nicely, I'll just say 'yes.'"

"Diane from work?"

His eyes flew open and he leaned in closer to Aubrey. His voice was an intense whisper. "Where did that name come from?"

"Are you seeing Diane from work?"

"None of your business."

"So, that's a 'yes' too."

"What's going on here, Aubrey? Did you see or hear something you should tell me about?"

"Is she here with you?"

"What? No. I'm here with Earl Cummings. He's probably still in the hotel bar celebrating his move up the ladder. Where did you hear about Diane? Your mother?"

"Promise you won't get mad. At me or her."

"I can't promise that, but you know me well enough to believe I can pretend quite well."

Now Aubrey's voice was as close to a whisper as the noisy crowd would allow. "Mom saw you together last week. She was really hurt."

"Why? Well, I suppose I can understand why she might be, but heckfire, we're divorced. I hope *she* starts dating again too."

"She thinks you had an affair with Diane. She thinks that's why you wanted the divorce."

His face hardened. "I'm only going to say this once. To you or her. I don't cheat and I don't lie. She knows that."

The front of the line was still dozens of people away. Aubrey looked straight down on a pair of twin boys putting on their ice skates while their parents looked on. She suddenly didn't need to go skating at Rockefeller Center. "We're going to be here forever, Dad. Let's just call it a day. I'm sure you have a flight to catch anyway."

"I'm sorry you have to go through this, sweetheart."

"I'm sorry I have to go through it too."

The Porters parted ways at Fifty-Second Street. Randall gave Aubrey a hug she only half-returned. He continued uptown and she turned south. When she hit Forty-Sixth, it started to snow. There was no wind, but the fine flakes swirled in the air stirred by people, cars, and busses. The snow darkened the sky just enough to trick some of the lights into coming on. White lights in the trees. Red and green lights in office building windows.

She stopped in front of a toy store. A giant bear dressed like Santa moved robot-like in the window as he gestured toward a dozen little elf bears. They were packing all manner of toys into an ornate sleigh. Aubrey could see through the back of the display into the store. Four or five children watched the action from inside.

She closed her eyes and turned her face to the sky. Gentle kisses of snow hit her face and forehead as the flakes got bigger. She knew she should be smiling. She should be celebrating. She should be *Christmasing*.

When she opened her eyes again, she looked right at a woman who had just come out of the store. She looked happy until her eyes locked onto Aubrey's. Her face fell and took on a look of sad compassion. *Is it that obvious?* Aubrey thought.

She hurried on. At the next block, she looked across the street just as a bus pulled through the intersection and revealed a vacant storefront. It was the alcove Aubrey had ducked into with Flare's camera gear. The place she'd been robbed. The place she sat on the ground while all her plans turned upside down.

She sat down next to a businessman on the bench where she'd met Jole. The man pulled his elbows in and gave her a scowl as he fiddled with his phone. He got up and left when the young woman next to him began to cry.

⌒☉

Why am I doing this to myself?

Tears streamed down Aubrey's cheeks and onto her keyboard as she sat at her desk and scrolled through twenty-three years of family photographs. For her parents' twentieth anniversary, she'd collected, organized and touched-up all the pictures her mother could put her hands on. Now she let them drag her through a rosebush of memories.

Claire and Randall didn't deliberately follow a pattern, but one clearly emerged when the pictures they took were strung together. The very first picture in the electronic stack was Aubrey as an infant in Claire's arms.

Then Aubrey's first Christmas.

Aubrey's first birthday.

The annual family vacation.

Aubrey's second Christmas.

And on and on. Images of other events were interspersed with birthdays and Christmases, but the consistency of those events made them stand out.

She collapsed the photos into screens full of small thumbnail images and selected only the Christmas pictures. She told the computer to create a slideshow with the music from "Christmas at Rockefeller Center" as the soundtrack.

A time-lapse movie of her life played on a fifteen-inch screen. Tinny music from the laptop speakers still managed to go right to her soul. The setting for each picture was the same.

A big Christmas tree with familiar family ornaments on it.

Mom in pajamas.

Aubrey in a new nightgown or footy pajamas she'd opened on Christmas Eve.

She was two years old and then three, four, five. Claire hardly changed at all, and Randall was behind the camera. In over a hundred pictures of more than twenty Christmases, he only appeared a few times.

Twelve-year-old Aubrey hugging Samantha the American Girl. *I don't believe I have ever been happier than I was at that moment,* she thought.

Fifteen-year-old Aubrey watching her father unwrap a hideous belt from Cavenders. *Did he ever wear that belt?*

Eighteen-year-old Aubrey pouting because her gifts weren't as extravagant as she'd expected.

She stopped the music and stepped backwards from last year's pictures and lingered on the photographs that included Claire or Randall. She thought she could see a woman playing the role of a happy mother on Christmas morning. As she moved back in time, the smiles got bigger and the eyes got clearer.

She filled the screen with a picture from the year 2000. Randall must have used the camera's timer because all three Porters were in it. The picture was terrible. They stood right in front of the tree and branches seemed to sprout from their heads. Their faces were slightly blurry because the camera had focused on the box Aubrey held. Randall had his arm around Claire's waist and she had her tilted head tucked under his chin. *They loved each other.* Claire had Aubrey wrapped in a one-armed embrace. *They loved me.*

It was the most beautiful picture of the set.

4 Days to Christmas

I have a surprise for you," Jole said over the phone.

"I hope it's a good one. It's been a rough week."

"Don't get too excited, but I think you'll like it."

"Okay . . ."

"Can you meet me at Times Square in an hour?"

"I guess so. Sure."

"Don't eat dinner. It's part of the surprise."

"Please tell me you are finally taking me to the Times Square TGI Friday!"

"You guessed so quick! No, Miss Snotty New Yorker, I am not taking you to the biggest tourist trap in Manhattan during the busiest week of the year."

"Phew."

"Bring your camera, too, if you don't mind. I'd like you to take some 'before' pictures."

"Before what?"

"That's part of the surprise."

"Awesome. See you in an hour . . . Wait! Times Square is a little big. Where should we meet?"

"How about the recruiting station?"

"See you there."

Aubrey didn't want to be late so she left a few minutes after hanging up. It was cold, but dry and calm, so she decided to walk the dozen blocks to Times Square. It seemed like half the city was walking along with her. The sidewalks were stuffed with heavy coats, thick scarves, knit caps, and ruddy faces. Every third person was carrying at least one shopping bag.

By the time she got to the recruiting station in the middle of the square, she was tired, cold, and cranky. Christmas shoppers moved so slowly. Only gawking tourists were worse. Worst of all were shopping gawking tourists.

"Merry Christmas!" Jole said from behind her.

"Hey."

"Let's go. Our dinner's getting cold." He took her gloved hand in his and led her down Forty-Third Street. They walked in silence and Aubrey could tell Jole was excited. His pace picked up as they neared a green awning with "Times Subs" printed on all three sides in gold lettering.

"They look closed, Jole."

"No, no, my dear. They just aren't *open* yet." He took off his gloves and fished a key ring out of his coat pocket. After opening the door, he held it for her and swept one arm across his body as he bowed like a maître d'.

The restaurant was lit only by the glowing EXIT sign toward the back. Jole fumbled for what Aubrey thought was a light switch, but when the room did light up, it was in the dim red and green of a string of Christmas lights. They were strung along the top edges of a booth. A pizza box from Anna's sat in the middle of the table, flanked by two paper plates and napkins.

I guess this is supposed to be romantic, Aubrey thought.

The Christmas lights did not have the effect on her she suspected Jole wanted them to. He slid in beside her.

"Very festive," she said.

"Isn't it? But aren't you wondering what we're doing eating not-so-warm pizza in an abandoned sub shop?"

"I just thought you were being an eccentric millionaire."

"Well, yeah, but there is a method to my madness." He paused for effect. "This is the newest location of Anna's New York Pizza!"

"Wow. That's awesome. Congratulations. When will it open?"

"In a few weeks, I hope. It takes forever to get all the permits and such but I greased the skids as much as I could. It helps that it was already an established restaurant."

"It's so close to Times Square. I'll bet you'll get a lot of tourist traffic."

"You don't know the half of it. Our internet promotion has been pulling people into the main store from all over the country. They make a special trip just to eat there. Now it'll be easier for us to be part of their New York experience. And there's more."

"More?"

"I . . . we . . . Francis and I . . . also picked up a place in your neighborhood. It will open even sooner because it's already a pizza restaurant."

"Bonds? Their pizza is terrible."

"Not for much longer. By spring, it will be another Anna's and will have the best slices in the city."

"Good for you guys. I'm so happy for you." She patted his arm.

"You don't seem too happy. What's going on?"

Half of Jole's face was lit red and the other was bathed in green light. More Christmas lights blinked on and off in the window of the store across the street. The pizza box in front of her had a wreath printed around the pizza and the label said, "Happy Holidays from Anna's." Christmas was everywhere except Aubrey's heart. "I'm having a bad week," she whispered. "A bad month, in fact."

Jole got up and found the switch. Christmas fled from the glaring white overhead lights. He sat down across from her. "Your parents."

"They're part of it. Most of it, I guess. This just isn't how it's supposed to be."

"How's it supposed to be?"

"I'm supposed to be a successful New York photographer. I know it's not automatic and I wouldn't be one by now anyway, but I'm headed the wrong direction." She felt the words build up in her chest and press against each other for the chance to escape. "I'm supposed to be having the best Christmas of my life in the best city in the world. I'm supposed to have two parents who live together and visit me together and tell me I'm going to be okay. I'm supposed to be a grown-up woman with a boyfriend and a job and friends." *Why am I not crying?* "I'm supposed to be happy . . . I suppose."

Jole looked at her for what seemed like a full minute without speaking. "How much of that can you control?"

"What?"

"How much of your perfect picture is in your control?"

"I don't know. Not much, I guess."

"Then why does it all bother you so much?"

"Are you saying I should just whistle a happy tune and pretend everything is fine?"

"No. I'm saying we get to decide how happy we are even if we don't get to decide what happens to us."

"You make it sound so easy," she said with just enough sarcasm for him to notice.

"You're the one who said it's important to see things differently. Take Christmas, for instance. You didn't have a lot of control over when your parents visited or what they did while they were here, but you did decide what *you* did and how *you* reacted. Nothing out there changed. The tree at Rock Center is the same. The decorations are the same. The kids running through FAO Schwartz are the same. You get to decide how to frame the picture, whether to smile or frown."

"This is beginning to sound a little bit like a lecture."

"I don't mean it to be, Aubrey. It is just hard to watch you put yourself through this. Don't you think Christmas could be hard for me? I'm completely estranged from my parents. I have few real friends here. My brain seems to be wired to always look for a new project or angle on somebody else's project. It's taking work for me to get the Christmas spirit. Heck, I'm not even sure what that is anymore."

Aubrey stood. Her knees almost buckled and she steadied herself on the back of the booth. She didn't know why, but she knew she had to get out of Times Subs as soon as she could. "I gotta go. Sorry."

"Don't. Aubrey, I'm trying to be a friend. I would love to enjoy the last few days before Christmas with you."

"I can't. I don't think I will ever enjoy any days of any Christmas ever again." She walked out of the restaurant without looking back at the only friend she had in New York City.

She gave her last cash to a cab driver to take her home. He took the scenic route. She kept her eyes closed the whole trip.

2 Days to Christmas

*A*ubrey didn't leave her apartment for two days except to buy some milk and ice cream. She spent her time organizing her computer without looking at any photographs. She surfed the internet. She dismantled the tree of gifts by the window and shoved the packages into the closet. She ordered Chinese. She half-heartedly looked at job postings. She tried not to think about Jole or the Porters.

Jole sent her several texts the first day. She ignored them. None came the second day.

For the first time since starting college, she didn't call her mother on Sunday. She didn't answer her call either.

On Monday morning, Aubrey's phone rang. A picture of her father with the name "Dad" underneath told her who was on the other end. Two minutes after she ignored it, she got a text.

Dad: Answer the phone. Worried. Will send police to check on you.

The phone rang again and she answered. "Hello."

"Are you okay? Your mom said she hasn't heard from you in days."

"I'm fine. Just busy."

"Busy. Busy with what, Aubrey? I called Flare to check on you and they told me you no longer worked there. When did that happen?"

"When did you start stalking me? I never told you where I worked."

"And now I know why. I'll answer your question, but that's not why we called. You posted a picture on Facebook in front of Flare New York Photography."

"Who's we?"

"Putting you on speaker. Still there?"

"Yes. Who's we?"

"It's me, dear," Claire answered from a tunnel.

"Hi, Mom. Sorry I didn't call yesterday. I was . . ."

". . . Busy," Randall finished. "Look, Aubrey, Claire and I got together and cleared the air between us."

Claire jumped in. "I'm so sorry, sweetheart. I jumped to the wrong conclusion. Your father has his faults, but I should never have believed he would be unfaithful."

"We talked for hours last night, honey," Randall added. "We thought we were saving you, protecting you, by holding off on the divorce. We were wrong."

"And I shouldn't have come up there and ruined your Christmas," Claire said.

"And I should have done a better job of separating business from family when I was there."

"So, let me see if I've got this straight," Aubrey said evenly. "*Now* you sit down and talk about what's right for me. *Now* you decide that hiding the truth wasn't best for me after all. *Now* you want everything to be okay."

"We were only thinking of you."

"Uh-huh."

"Careful, Aubrey." Randall shifted into patriarch mode. "Remember that this affects all of us. Claire is devastated and it hasn't exactly been a walk in the park for me either."

Aubrey began to get the same full feeling she had at the sub shop with Jole. She could feel her face begin to flush. Most of her knew that she should just accept the apology and take time to collect herself. Most of her knew that her parents were trying. The small and exhausted part of her that controlled the floodgates holding back years of pain and uncertainty took control and then stepped aside. "Don't tell me to be careful. Don't tell me you were thinking of me. If you'd been 'thinking of me,' you wouldn't have lied to me for, what, ten years? Or is it fifteen? Twenty? Was it all fake? Were you ever happily married?"

"Aubrey . . ."

"I'm not done. This is the worst year of my life. The worst Christmas. You know why I never told you where I worked, Dad? Because I knew it wouldn't be good enough for you. I didn't tell Mom because I didn't need her patting me on the head. Ever since I was a kid, almost every decision I made was to make you happy or proud. Turns out I was wasting my time."

A hand—Randall's most likely—covered the phone. Aubrey listened to muffled voices. They were discussing, not arguing. When Randall finally spoke, it was with a calmness that surprised Aubrey. Claire cried in the background. "We don't know what to say. You need to figure out what to do next. You will always be our daughter, but you're obviously not our little girl anymore. We hope you'll see things differently soon. We love you." Claire's sobbing almost drowned out Randall's soliloquy.

Aubrey wanted to cry, but was far too spent. She took the phone from her ear, looked down at her father's picture, and ended the call.

Christmas Eve

*E*ven Santa Claus was telling Aubrey Christmas was not worth the pain and stress. She watched two cops try to calm a drunk, presumably homeless man who was wearing a red fleece cap with a puffy, formerly white but now city-gray ball at its point. He was also wearing a fake Santa beard that didn't begin to cover his own scruffy growth.

"C'mon, Santa. You can either join your elves at the shelter or spend the night in lockup with somebody on your naughty list."

"I'm not Santa! Why you callin' me Santa? Just leave me alone. I ain't botherin' nobody."

"Look, pal, you've had too much nog and not enough egg. You've got to move along."

Aubrey wanted to use her phone to capture the scene, but New York's Finest aren't the most camera-friendly people when they are working. Instead, she walked around them, stepping off the curb and into a slushy gutter. "Awesome," she said to her wet sneakers.

She walked into the bodega and was surprised to see a few other customers. It was Christmas Eve, after all, and the streets were beginning to empty. This particular establishment, cleverly named "The Grocery," had remained blessedly free of Christmas cheer. The few times over the past couple of days she had left her apartment, Aubrey walked four extra blocks every time she needed to buy something. The place nearest her apartment looked like it belonged at the North Pole. It was also right next to the future Chelsea location of Anna's Pizza.

The owners of "The Grocery" must have gotten a good deal on Chinese Christmas kitsch since Aubrey's last visit. It wasn't as bad as other stores, but a string of lights (2 for $5) ran along the top of the snack shelf. Christmas music drifted quietly out of an ancient radio/cassette/CD player on the counter. She ignored them and walked quickly to the back to grab a rotisserie chicken.

As she picked up the plastic container, the air around it stirred and sent a mixture of scents through Aubrey's nose and deep into her memory. The chicken was a turkey sitting on a dining table so polished that "passing the potatoes" involved giving the bowl a gentle push and watching it glide to the next person. Other smells from the deli section combined to recreate a Christmas dinner in the Porter household when a little girl named Aubrey had everything she could imagine wanting.

She pushed against the emotions moving from her memory to her chest. The radio began to play "I'll Be Home for Christmas" and the clerk turned up the volume. Her eyes began to burn as she did not cry. She put her chicken on the counter and focused on getting to her wallet. Her gaze shifted from her messenger bag to the glass case in front of her. All of the souvenirs that usually filled the space had been replaced with a beautiful, simple Nativity set. Baby Jesus was perfectly formed from brilliant porcelain. His tiny arms were outstretched, reaching for someone.

He looked at her.

Aubrey took a deep breath and tried to regain her composure. She was a New Yorker who hated Christmas. Hated Christmas and all it represented. Biting the inside of her cheek, she slid her purchase along the glass and finally looked toward the clerk behind the register.

The old man—the owner, probably—was leaning over with his hairy forearms resting on the counter. He had just turned off the radio and was talking quietly to a little girl. They were both looking at a tabletop Christmas tree sitting next to the register. He flipped a switch on its base and what seemed like a thousand tiny colored bulbs lit the bushy, plastic branches. The angel on top of the tree began to rotate as a tinny version of "Angels We Have Heard on High" filled the air.

Big Aubrey felt herself begin to lose control of little Aubrey. She blinked quickly a few times and took out her phone to see if something or someone could distract her. When she unlocked the screen, the phone resumed the last app she'd used: the camera. It was aimed at the little girl. Aubrey reflexively composed a shot of a dark-haired six-year-old looking with innocent wonder at a cheap plastic Christmas tree.

The girl turned and looked at Aubrey. Their dark brown eyes met and Aubrey saw herself.

The girl smiled.

The woman choked back a sob.

"Why are you sad?"

"I'm not sure."

"But it's Christmas!"

"I know," Aubrey managed to whisper.

"Isn't it wonderful?!"

Aubrey, suddenly and miraculously free of the resentment and anger she'd been wearing like Jacob Marley's chains, turned away from the little girl and toward the display case. She thought about all the people who were waiting to love her. She decided to let them.

"Yes. It's wonderful."

"Merry Christmas, lady."

"Merry Christmas."

Christmas Day

*A*ubrey Porter was five again. She woke up every hour after falling into an exhausted sleep after midnight. The pure joy and excitement she felt made it impossible for her to stay asleep. But there was nothing more she could do until at least six or seven.

"Mommy? Daddy?" she remembered saying, "Is it time?"

"No, honey, Santa hasn't come yet," Claire answered.

"He's still in China," Randall added.

"Oh. How much longer?"

"Come back when it's light enough for you to see the swing set outside your window."

The memory made Aubrey smile as she dozed off again.

She awoke at six and managed to stay in bed until the morning twilight made the streetlight outside her window turn off. She dressed, gathered her things, and left the apartment. A lot of the preparation was now out of her hands. She could only hope her friends— old and new—had done what she'd asked, begged, and cajoled them into.

As she walked the last block to her destination, she imagined the conversation Francis and Jole would be having any minute. "Jole," Francis would say, "we've got a problem at the Chelsea location. Somebody broke in. The cops need somebody down there. Can you go? I've got my brother and his family here."

Jole would, Aubrey hoped, agree, even if he was a little cranky about it. His decision was one of a dozen things that had to go exactly right for this Christmas to work according to plan.

She put the key Francis had given her the night before into the lock and gave it a hopeful turn. Stepping inside, she quickly punched in the code to disarm the alarm system and was relieved when the light turned green. *Two more hurdles cleared.*

Everything was just as she'd left it the night before. She went to the kitchen and hoped she could remember the instructions Francis had given her in a rush of New York English. As she opened the giant refrigerator to gather her ingredients, she glanced at the ancient clock above the cook's station. *Seven-thirty. I'd better hustle.*

She made it just in time. Breakfast was under the warming lights, and the giant apron she'd had to adjust with clothespins was back on its hook. Now she sat in the darkened restaurant, hoping she didn't have Bisquick in her hair.

Her heart began sounding in her ears as Jole stopped in front of the glass door. He looked left and right, clearly confused at the lack of policemen. He finally opened the door, but did not step inside when he saw the alarm was not set.

"Hello?" he said tentatively.

"Merry Christmas!" Aubrey answered as she flipped the switch on the outlet strip that had a plug in every slot. Instantly, the room erupted into Christmas. Just inside the door stood an eight-foot-tall blue spruce tree decorated from top to bottom with lights and every ornament Aubrey could find. She had made the guy closing up his Christmas tree lot and the owners of a half-dozen convenience stores extremely happy. The gifts Claire bought, along with a dozen others, filled the space under the lowest branches.

Strings of lights and long lengths of shimmering garland ran along and across the room.

A shocked, unshaven Jole Muller stood in the doorway with his mouth hanging open. Aubrey was afraid he might turn and run. She was relieved when he stepped inside and closed the door behind him. "Aubrey?"

"That's me."

"What is all this?"

"It's Christmas. Sit down. I made breakfast."

He sat where she gestured. "I don't get it. I mean it's nice, but I don't get it."

"There's nothing to get. That's what a little girl taught me yesterday."

He scooted over so she could sit next to him. She explained, "Christmas is magic to little kids. It just happens and they get to enjoy it. It's all about them. I've been trying to make it all about me this year, but I forgot something very important."

"What's that?"

"It works for kids because *somebody else* is making it all about them. Christmas works when people forget themselves and give to others." She laughed as she heard her complicated thoughts come out in such simple words. "You'd think an adult woman would know that by now, wouldn't you?"

"Don't be so hard on yourself. The world is full of old kids - and not in the good, innocent way. I'm happy for you that you see things differently."

Aubrey looked up at the clock. "Let's eat. We're on a tight schedule."

"Do I have any say in this schedule?" he asked with a grin.

"Not really."

Just as they were finishing their French toast, pancakes, and scrambled eggs, Aubrey's phone chirped to tell her she had a new text message.

Outside house. Standing by.

A few seconds later, another text hit from another number.

I'm here. Ready 2 go.

"I need to borrow your phone, Jole."

He handed it over without saying anything. She composed a text message to both numbers, but didn't hit "send." Then she dialed a number on her own phone.

"Hello?"

"Mom? It's me, Aubrey."

"Aubrey? Aubrey! I'm so glad you called. Merry Christmas."

"Hold on just a minute, Mom." She put Claire on hold and dialed a second number.

"Hello."

"Dad?"

"Aubrey?"

"Yeah." She touched her phone. "Mom? You still there?"

"Yes, dear. What's . . ."

"Dad, you there?"

"I'm here."

"I'm putting you both on speaker." She hit "send" on Jole's phone. "First, you'd better answer your door."

She grinned smugly at Jole as the sound of door-bells came over the speaker. They could hear Randall and Claire each talking to someone. "Thank you. Merry Christmas to you too."

Aubrey waited a few seconds and then asked, "Are you back?"

"What's this all about, Aubrey? How did you . . . what did you do?" Claire asked.

"You should each be holding a gift from me. I want you to open it at the same time. On three. Ready? One, two, three."

Papers shuffled. Aubrey could pick out which sounds came from Randall and which were from Claire. One was two quick rips; the other was careful. Aubrey could imagine her mother carefully slipping her finger under the tape, removing the picture and then setting the wrapping aside for future folding. She heard Claire begin to cry softly.

"Do you remember that picture?" Aubrey said.

Simultaneous "yesses" came over the line. She put the same photo on the table in front of Jole. It was the one of the Porters hugging each other on a Christmas morning.

"That's a picture of the Porter family many years ago. We changed after that." She paused. "We *all* changed. It doesn't matter how it happened. It's nobody's fault. We're a different family now. But, I hope we can still be a family."

"Of course," Randall said.

Claire said nothing.

"Mom?"

After several disconcerting seconds, Aubrey's mother answered, "Oh, sweetheart. This is the best Christmas ever."

"I forgot to tell you something really important," Aubrey said as she looked over at Jole. "I'm here with a friend. His name is Jole."

They all visited for a few minutes and then said goodbye and Merry Christmas. "What a great Christmas morning," Jole said. "Thanks for letting me be part of it."

"It's not over yet. We haven't opened our presents." She took him by the hand and led him over to the tree. "Most of these are to me from my Mom." She took a rectangular package and handed it to Jole. "This one is for you."

He started to open it while still looking at a grinning Aubrey. "A photo album?"

"Open it."

He opened the front cover and then turned past the front blank page. And then he seemed to lose his balance. He sank into a hard metal restaurant chair. "Where . . . how did you get these?"

Of all the things that had to go just right, this one had the most risk. "Your mom." She held her breath.

"How?"

"It wasn't too hard to find a Dr. Muller who teaches women's studies at Stanford. She answered my email right away."

"Did you . . . does she . . . ?"

"No. I just told her I was a friend putting together a last-minute Christmas gift. She doesn't know where you are." She put a hand on his face. "She wants to, though."

His eyes were glistening, but he remained composed. "Thank you. Thank you so much." He stood up and embraced her hard.

"You're welcome."

"I have something for you too. I was actually afraid I wouldn't get a chance to give it to you. It's back at my apartment."

"Jole, just tell me you haven't given up on me. That's all the Christmas I need."

He pulled her back in and kissed her.

Epilogue

Aubrey's fortunes changed along with her attitude. Tyrone saw the collection of Christmas window display photos she'd posted online. He showed them to his bosses at Flare without telling them the pictures were taken by an intern they'd fired. By the end of January, Aubrey had a job offer as a junior photographer.

She didn't start her new job until the middle of February because she spent two weeks back in Texas. She formed a new bond with her mother that left them closer than ever. She didn't have quite the same experience with Randall, but she did get to know Diane and returned to New York on good terms with everyone.

Her career as a staff photographer lasted less than a year. In the late summer, Jole hired his brand new fiancée to be the creative director of a new online photography services business. Tyrone came on board as the office manager, herder of interns, and wedding planner.

Francis and Jole sold the Anna's New York Pizza franchise to a major restaurant chain. Part of Francis's compensation was full and autonomous ownership of his original shop.

Aubrey spent the next Christmas in Texas.

Jole spent it in California.

They both carried the picture of a little girl staring with wonder at a cheap plastic musical Christmas tree with an angel on top spinning in circles.

About the Authors

Jason Wright is a *New York Times* bestselling author, motivational speaker, and writing consultant. He's also a columnist for *Fox News* and *The Deseret News*. Articles by Jason have appeared in over fifty newspapers and magazines.

Jason is the author of *The James Miracle, Christmas Jars, The Wednesday Letters, Recovering Charles, Christmas Jars Reunion, Penny's Christmas Jar Miracle, The Cross Gardener, The Seventeen Second Miracle, The Wedding Letters, The 13th Day of Christmas, Picturing*

Christmas, The James Miracle: 10th Anniversary Edition, Christmas Jars Journey, A Letter to Mary, and the upcoming children's novel, *The Lost Carnival.*

Jason lives in Virginia's Shenandoah Valley with his wife, Kodi Erekson Wright. They have two girls, two boys, and a 110-pound Goldendoodle named Pilgrim who thinks he's a lapdog.

SCAN TO VISIT

HTTP://JASONFWRIGHT.COM

You may have read something by Sterling Wright without even knowing it. He has collaborated on several novels, including a *New York Times* bestseller. "Picturing Christmas" is the first—but not the last—novel published under his own name. He and his wife make their home in beautiful central Virginia.